FIC Worboys

Worboys, Anne.

Hotel girl /

HOTEL GIRL

A Selection of Recent Titles by Anne Worboys

ALICE

A KINGDOM FOR THE BOLD

THE LION OF DELOS

RUN, SARA, RUN *

SEASON OF THE SENSES *

VILLAGE SINS *

* *available from Severn House*

HOTEL GIRL

Anne Worboys

This first world edition published in Great Britain 1997 by
SEVERN HOUSE PUBLISHERS LTD of
9–15 High Street, Sutton, Surrey SM1 1DF.
First published in the USA 1997 by
SEVERN HOUSE PUBLISHERS INC., of
595 Madison Avenue, New York, NY 10022.

British Library Cataloguing in Publication Data

Worboys, Anne
      Hotel Girl
      1. Romantic Suspense novels
      1. Title
      823.9'14 [F]

      ISBN 0-7278-5197-7

Typeset by Palimpsest Book Production Limited,
Polmont, Stirlingshire, Scotland.
Printed and bound in Great Britain by
Hartnolls Ltd, Bodmin, Cornwall.

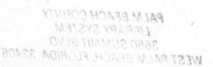

Chapter One

Paris. It was three weeks until their wedding date. Julie and Martin were having a quiet dinner at a little restaurant in the Rue de Richelieu, a block away from Julie's family hotel. His tawny eyes roved over her thick blonde hair that lay on her shoulders and gave a faintly unreal look to her dark, feathery brows; over her wide cheekbones and pointed chin. His long legs under the narrow table pressed against hers. They were well matched, both tall and slender. Both fair.

"Tonight I'm going to share my plans with you," he said. "Husbands and wives shouldn't have secrets from each other."

She smiled at him, at his boyish enthusiasm. And then he dropped the bombshell.

"As soon as we're safely married and all this business is tied up I'm going back into antiques. You'll like that, won't you Julie? You like antiques."

She could only put her fork down and stare at him in consternation, wondering if she knew him, this man she was going to marry.

"Now our parents have settled their differences and all the papers are signed for the hotel amalgamation I'm going to take out a mortgage and buy you a mansion in the English countryside. Somewhere not too far from London. We'll furnish it with the best antiques I can buy," Martin said.

"Martin!"

He mistook her shock for surprise. "We'll advertise through the fine furniture magazines. Entertain rich clients. We'll wine and dine them, then show them over the house. We'll sell them the chairs they've been sitting on." His fairish brows drew together, the tawny eyes sharpened.

"Why are you looking like that, Julie? Isn't this right up your alley? You could do flower arrangements to set off the furniture. Some people haven't a clue about – well – all the things you and I are good at. Decorating. Matching up *objets d'art*. Choosing pictures. We'll make it easy for them. We'll sell them entire furnished rooms."

Martin leaned across the tiny table on which lay a little wreath of lilies-of-the-valley because the restaurant owner knew they were to be married. He touched Julie's long, silky gold hair and told her, as she recoiled in dismay, "You'll be an ornament for my shop window. One of my greatest assets. The only one not for sale." He laughed.

Martin Wingate was blond, thin, clever. Antiques had been his passion ever since his mother, who spoiled him, gave him a Georgian desk when he left school. He had told Julie when they first began going out together that it was his ambition to sell antiques internationally. "I, too, can be a jet setter," he said with a sly smile, referring to the fact that her parents owned hotels in London, Paris and Geneva. "I've got a friend in Hollywood who wants me to export them over there. Perhaps you could fix me up with contacts on the Continent."

She remembered protesting that English antiques should stay at home. "They'll come back," he replied carelessly. "It's just business."

She hadn't liked that, but put it aside. It was, after all, because of his great love of antiques that Julie had thought so much of him when he gave them up to please his father and opted to go into the hotel business.

As an only child, she thought, loving him for his kindness, he was bound to inherit the hotel anyway.

It wasn't difficult, she thought afterwards, looking back, for her admiration, fed by Martin's charm, to grow into love. And there had been the added pleasure of delighting her parents. The Silvine, a brash glass and concrete monstrosity in the West End was worth every bit as much as the Creighton's three hotels put together.

Julie was glad for both families, that Martin's and her love affair had brought their parents together. She didn't know why they had not always been friends, except that they were very different men. The one, brash, *nouveau riche*, ruthlessly ambitious, the other a gentle man who had inherited his wealth, who had hoped for a son to take over. Their son had died in infancy, leaving Julie to compensate.

Martin cast the matter of their parents' differences aside in his lighthearted way, saying her father was jealous because Oliver Wingate owned one of the most popular hotels in London. He added quickly that his own father was jealous of Neil Creighton's owning three in three different countries.

"We've got more business," he said at the time, his eyes glinting, "but you're superior and jet set. Old school stuff," he said, pretending to scoff, looking at Julie with mischief in his eyes. "With the amalgamation, they've got it made. It remains only for them to get on, and that's up to them."

Now, horrified at the way Martin had tricked her father and his, Julie stared at him in disbelief. "You broke your word!"

His thin face darkened. "I merely manipulated our parents into settling their differences. I did them a good turn."

"Martin!"

"What do you mean, 'Martin'?" he asked roughly. "Hasn't everyone got what they wanted?" He had a wide mouth, mobile in laughter. Now it hardened into a line straight as a railway track.

She leaned towards him, looking up entreatingly into his hostile face. "Your father – and mine – are relying on you. There's a job to be done. They're counting on us both to help." Already there were structural alterations going ahead on the roof of the Hotel Merrion in London where she and Martin were to live. Generously, Julie's father had offered them the tiny penthouse.

Martin brushed her protest aside. "They'll find someone. There are dozens – hundreds of people looking for a responsible job in hotel management."

"They wanted you! A member of the family. That's what the amalgamation was all about. You know that."

"If they pay enough they'll find someone they can rely

on," Martin retorted carelessly. His mouth turned up at the corners again. "Why should we allow ourselves to be used? If two grown men can't get on, that's their problem. If they feel strongly enough about the amalgamation, they'll jolly well make the effort."

And that was true enough, Julie had to admit, even while she contained her anxiety, listening to the hurried beating of her heart. She could not believe that he would just stand by and allow their fathers to arrange things that were too complex, too family-orientated to be handed over to a stranger, then do this. Yet she was going to promise to love, honour and cherish this man. A man she suddenly realised she could not trust and did not know.

Afterwards, as they sat in his fast little sports car, before driving home, Julie said miserably, "Martin, I have to think about this."

"About what?" But he knew. It was in the coldness behind his eyes.

Fear and dread made her say what had to be said. "I've seen a different side of you tonight. I didn't know . . . I'm not certain I could live with . . ."

"What are you trying to say?" he demanded. He leaned away from her, frowning down into her face.

She braced herself. "I thought I was marrying an honest man."

His eyes were bright with anger. She felt his hard hand on her wrist, the fingers tightening. "You're marrying a businessman," he said.

"If that's your idea of business . . . " she said. She saw his withdrawal and panicked. "Martin, I have to think. Give me time."

"Until tomorrow morning?" he asked roughly, angrily. "That's the time I'll give you."

Inside her disordered brain a quiet, oddly calm voice was saying, 'There's been a dreadful mistake. The man you love doesn't exist, Julie.'

Martin let out the clutch and the little car shot into the traffic. They drove in stony silence, stony on Martin's side, a silence pitted with horror on Julie's. At the front door of the Hôtel le Sceptre on the Rue St.-Jean he braked. "Well?"

She could not answer. All she could think was that the wedding was arranged. It could not be cancelled. Four hundred guests! A cream silk taffeta dress, a Brussels lace veil! How could she let down all those friends of her family?

And then Georges, the commissionaire, was opening the door of the car. "Mademoiselle?"

She turned to Martin, all the anguish, the confusion, the fear of the future in her face. "Martin . . . ?" Suddenly in an icy voice, he was telling her an address. "I'm going to see Antonia. If you want me, you'll find me there." He flung the words at her. Her mind went blank. She had not been able to take in this second shock coming so fast on the heels of the first.

"Antonia?" she echoed stupidly. No. That was all over. A part of another life. Antonia did not exist any more. And then with disbelief, she read the truth in Martin's angry eyes. Antonia did exist. Had always done so. He must have brought her to Paris! Now, at the first breath of disruption, he was going to her like a homing pigeon. Or had he been with her all through their engagement . . . ?

Julie sat looking at the stranger beside her and knew with a terrible clarity that there was going to be no wedding. The details no longer mattered. The car door was open. She looked up into the commissionaire's kindly, concerned face, then she stepped out and the low-slung sports car roared away.

She crossed the foyer avoiding the eyes of the smiling staff, the English Harry who had come over from the Merrion at the desk, Jacques the hovering waiter with his white napkin and silver tray and went up in the lift to the penthouse that was the family home. She was close to tears as she opened the door.

Her mother looked up from her *gros point*. She was a small woman, softly curved, with Julie's fair hair that was lightly permed and well cut so that it flicked up over her ears. She wore a hostess gown of yellow cotton. Julie thought of

5

hostess gowns as her mother's trademark. They came in different materials and were differently patterned. What they had in common was that they hung straight from her shoulders and hid her comfortable house shoes, or even slippers. They were Delia Creighton's answer to the public life she was obliged to lead. She had a wardrobe of them. When she tired of one, which was seldom, she gave it to Oxfam and bought another.

She had never worked. Never even taken much interest in the family business. Not that that was her fault. Her husband had wanted to make a pet of her. "Leave it to me," he would say, and she had been happy to do so. Julie thought her parents had the perfect marriage.

She looked round the comfortable drawing room with its velvet sofas and deep chairs. She took a deep breath and announced boldly, "I'm not going to marry Martin." Was that panic in her mother's eyes, swiftly hidden?

"But it's all arranged," she said.

"It's going to have to be unarranged," Julie retorted before recognising it was not the reply her mother expected.

Her mother's eyes glazed over. Then, "Is this about Antonia?" she asked.

Julie frowned. "What do you mean?"

Delia hauled herself off the sofa. "I think I'd better get your father." Her voice sounded distinctly panicky.

"No." Julie moved into her path. "No." She had a feeling of being trapped, and not just by the proposed marriage. "I want you to tell me," she said. "First things first. What do you know about Antonia?"

Delia's eyes clouded. "Oh darling, we didn't want you to hear. She wrote to me."

"When?"

"After the announcement of your engagement to Martin."

"Did you keep the letter?"

"Yes."

"Please show it to me. I cannot imagine why you didn't show it to me before."

"It was for the best," her mother said. "It seemed for the best, at the time. We decided not—"

"Mother," Julie cut in, "let me be the judge of what is best for me."

Her mother looked close to tears. "Don't be angry, dear."

"I am angry. You're playing around with my life. Show me the letter, Mother."

The stairs to the upper floor led out of the drawing room. The pinkish mushroom carpet followed through. Julie, watching her mother's back, wondered if she should have gone with her in case she destroyed the letter. But why should she? The time to do that was the day it arrived. She thought about the amalgamation of the hotels. Told herself she must not. Not until this business about Antonia was dealt with. But she did. The look on her mother's face had shaken her. Snatches of conversation kept diving into her mind. 'With you and Martin in charge . . .' Now she realised she had heard that phrase too often. How important was this marriage to the parents? Was it, in fact, essential? Was her father acceding to the amalgamation only because Julie was going to have a foot in the Wingate camp?

She cast her mind back to the evening she and Martin had met. The families had been dining at adjacent tables in a London restaurant. By chance, she had thought. But had it been by chance? She remembered the pleasure on the faces of both sets of parents when they introduced their children. She remembered the waiters being asked to move them to a bigger table that would accommodate six. Remembered Martin and herself being put together. Remembered falling for Martin's good looks and his charm.

Now she wondered if in fact that meeting had been engineered. Oliver Wingate and her father had never been friends.

Her mother came back down the stairs carrying the letter. She handed it over, still in its envelope. Julie opened out the single sheet. It was short. Little more than a note. It was written on plain paper in neat script.

"You had better tell your daughter," it began, "before she begins making wedding plans, that I've no intention of letting Martin go. And nor will he let me go. Even if she marries him, he will come back to me. He only wants her because she can be useful to him. He doesn't love her the way he loves me."

Useful to him! What could Antonia mean? That their marriage would make the amalgamation of the hotels possible? Or the fact that he would in time inherit their three properties? She folded the letter and put it back in the envelope. "Why didn't you show it to me before?"

"I thought it wasn't important."

"Not important!" Julie couldn't believe her ears.

"The idle threat of a jealous woman. You surely don't believe what she says. Why would he want to marry you if he loved her?"

"The letter is quite explicit," Julie replied. "He wants to marry me because I can be of use to him."

"If you believe it."

Julie's brain was turning over fast. She had been involved with the hotels all her working life. She had every intention of continuing to work after the marriage. It made sense that her parents would see her as a watch-dog.

"She had to have some excuse for writing such a dreadful letter," Delia said, dismissing it. "She had to give some reason. I should think it's all lies."

"It is not all lies," said Julie. "I'm sorry to say it is not. Antonia is here. Martin had gone to her place. Like a homing pigeon. You may think it bizarre but it is true that Martin brought Antonia over here. He brought his mistress with him when he came to Paris to see me and talk about the wedding. That is a fact, Mother, and you must believe it. And it's true," she continued, "what Antonia writes. He now stands to inherit our three hotels as well as the Silvine."

"Julie, dear," her mother protested, "why should he look at his marriage that way? You're being unfair. In any alliance there is give and take. You're doing well, too, in marrying him. He could say you're marrying him to get the Silvine."

"Mother!"

"Really, Julie. I'm only trying to put things in perspective. This is a good marriage for both of you."

Julie wanted to say, Yes, it would have been if you two had liked and trusted Oliver Wingate, but that was to accuse her parents of using her. She said, "I had a right to see this letter. You have let me down. Martin has not given Antonia up. If I had known what Antonia had to say I could have investigated before."

Her mother begged tearfully, "Please let me get Neil. He's in his study. Please."

Julie said grimly, "I'm going to make myself a cup of coffee." She was going to have to face her father some time. It may as well be now. She went into the kitchen and put the kettle on.

They did not come immediately. She wondered cynically if they were working out what to say. She had never before felt like this about her parents. But then, she thought, I was never aware of being used before. She had willingly gone into the hotel business, not only because her parents wanted her to, but because hotels had always been a part of her life. She had worked hard during her training for hotel management and since coming into the business she had given her undivided attention to her job. She had given a great deal.

And then, she reminded herself as she sipped the comforting coffee, she had to remember how privileged she was. How much her parents had given her. She looked round the kitchen, at the top-of-the-range cooker, the marble shelfing, everything of the very best. She went to the door of the big, opulent drawing room and stood looking in at the velvet floor-length drapes, the Persian carpet, the grand piano kept mainly for decoration, and told herself that if they saw her marrying Martin as a form of giving back, could she blame them? Yes, she said to herself sternly, she could. They have a perfect marriage. Why should they wish anything less on me?

She finished the coffee and went back to the drawing room to wait. Her father came in from the study door that opened off a small passage by the stairs. He was a very English looking man, tall and, aristocratic looking, with a soldierly bearing. In his youth he had been in a Guards regiment. He had

9

light blue eyes. His thinning fair hair was a little untidy now, as though in an absorbed moment he had flattened it down with his palms. He was wearing a plum-coloured dressing gown over pyjamas. There were slippers on his bare feet.

"Hello Julie," he said looking at her sternly as though it was she who had committed the wrong. "Give me that woman's address. I'll bring Martin back."

"Oh Father!" She laughed wryly with tears in her eyes.

"What do you mean, 'Oh Father'?"

"I mean, how can a man be so unworldly in the twentieth century? Besides, I don't want him back. I'm sure you've heard it all from Mother. He's been cheating me. I can't marry a cheat. And I can't share a husband, which is what this letter seems to infer I would have to do."

"If you love him," ventured her mother, "you could look on this as a little upset."

"There has been a mistake," Julie said bleakly. "I loved the man I thought he was. And I'm sorry. I see now what I didn't see clearly enough before. My marriage to Martin, in view of an amalgamation of the Wingates' and the Creightons' hotels would be, at the very least, convenient, at best, a miracle. You don't like each other. You don't trust Martin's father. I was to be your watch-dog, wasn't I? I see it now."

"Julie, you take a very harsh line."

"I'm feeling harsh," she retorted. "I don't like being used. If you and Oliver Wingate don't like each other, then forget about having business dealings. I am not prepared to be your spy."

"Julie, how can you talk like that to your father? It's not true. Oliver and Neil have settled their differences. I cannot imagine why you're talking like this. It's not true. Tell her it's not true, Neil."

He put an arm round Delia's shoulders.

Julie thought she had her answer. Her heart was heavy. "I don't blame you," she said, though she did.

"If I may say so, your view is rather a stark one my dear," her father said. "You're over-reacting. When you calm down I believe you'll see things in a better light."

Perhaps she was. Perhaps she would. She didn't like what she saw in their faces.

"Certainly you will have a foot in both businesses, but so will Martin." He attempted a smile. "You omitted to note that Martin will be watching our side of the business to see we don't step out of line."

"Martin isn't going to work in the hotel business." She told them what she had heard from him over dinner. "That's what he's going to do. Sell antiques."

Her father considered for a moment. "That's not a bad idea, as a side-line," he said. "Why shouldn't he have a hobby?"

"I mean," she said distinctly, "that is going to be his business. He's only going to be a name on the hotel letterhead."

"Oh, what nonsense." Her father brushed her words aside. "Martin has a big responsibility. His father is counting on him taking over in due course."

"What I am saying is that Martin isn't honest. He hasn't told his father what he's doing. He thought I would go into the antique business with him. His plan is that neither of us will work in the hotels. That leaves you and his father working together. Don't you see?"

Her father looked baffled. "I simply don't understand," he said.

"Then you had better talk to his father. But it involves spilling the beans about the antiques."

Neil looked uncertain. "I don't think I can interfere there. What I would like to talk to him about is this woman."

"No. That's between Martin and me. I've told him I'll let him know my decision in the morning. I'm going to have to say it's all off. I'm sorry. I'm very sorry it's turned out this way. But even if you had told me the amalgamation was dependent on our marriage I don't see it would have made any difference. I might simply have been frightened off earlier. I don't think I'd have wanted the responsibility."

"It wasn't dependent—" her father began, then broke off.

Go on, Julie wanted to say. She waited.

11

Her mother burst into tears. Again, Julie felt her mother had given her her answer. Her father stalked off to bed.

She did not have to get in touch with Martin. He arrived at the hotel at eight o'clock in the morning with a big bouquet of red roses in his arms. Julie did not invite him to come up. She descended to the foyer where people were coming and going. Martin would not dare make a scene there.

"Can't we talk privately?" he asked, looking hurt.

"I don't have any private business with you," she said ignoring the roses he was thrusting under her nose. "Not since you have spent the night with another woman. I just have to say the wedding is off."

He protested, half laughing, "Julie, I have friends. Antonia is one of them. I needed a bed last night. You didn't offer me one," he said outrageously.

She looked at his laughing mouth, his tawny eyes beneath the soft fair hair and realised she was still in love with him. She said, "Come over here." She led him to the far corner of the lounge, threading her way between the leather sofas and chairs. She sat down and took Antonia's letter out of her pocket. Martin read it in silence, then tore it up.

He looked at her with an endearing smile on his face. "Let's start again," he said, as though the letter had never been.

She leaned foward in her seat, looking into his eyes. "And you'll never see Antonia again?"

He gave an explosive little laugh tinged with outrage. "You want to take me over and get rid of all my friends?"

"Only one, Martin," she said, still watching him closely. "Only Antonia."

"You come first," he said warmly, lifting one of her hands, holding it between his own. "You will always be first, Julie darling, but I must have friends."

She couldn't believe he was saying this. She felt as though she was talking to a being from another planet. "And yet, you invited her over here. You must have found a flat for her. Why?"

"I told you. She is a friend. I would do that for any good friend. She has been very good to me."

12

"And had you invited her to the wedding?"

"You saw our list. You sent the invitations."

She thought he was having a game with her. It was in his laughing eyes. Why should she think he would invite Antonia to the wedding? She had the answer. Because the new Martin who was a virtual stranger to her was into tricks. She did not know Antonia's surname so could not check the list. She did not wish to know if he had played this little game of bringing his mistress to the wedding. Of humiliating his bride whilst saying, "Nonsense. You should not feel humiliated. She is a friend."

Why am I thinking like this? Because he did not give her a straight answer. He did not say 'No'. She saw then what she should have seen before: that Martin was not into straight answers. She recognised it as a part of his charm.

She tried to put Antonia behind her. "There's something I would like to know. Perhaps you can tell me why my parents should be so upset that this marriage isn't going to take place."

He looked thoughtful, and serious. "I'd be upset if I had organised a wedding and—"

"No, Martin," Julie said evenly. "I have done the organising. And I will do the cancelling. Give me the truth."

Again he appeared to ponder. Then, "Your father's not much of a businessman, is he, let's face it," he said. "The decorating that's going on was my father's idea. Not his. It's no longer OK to be genteel and slightly down-at-heel—"

She started to ask what decorating he was referring to, she had not heard of it, but her indignation overrode the question, "Our hotels are not down-at-heel." Her glance took in the comfortable brown sofas and chairs, the occasional tables of polished oak. The hard-wearing Axminster carpet that certainly was not new, but could hardly be said to need replacing. The walls were panelled, ageless and dignified, adorned with Old Master prints and here and there a carefully chosen modern original.

"Compared to the Silvine they are."

"I would not compare any of them with the Silvine," Julie flashed.

"Take these roses, Miss Haughty," said Martin thrusting them into her arms, laughing, "and let me soften you up with a kiss before you start calling my father Flash Harry."

She held the roses, looking over the top of them into Martin's teasing eyes. She was aware of people drifting through the lounge. Of curious stares. "Were you marrying me for the hotels?"

"Oh, Julie darling." He looked sincere, and hurt. "I am still marrying you, but not for the hotels. You know what I'm interested in. Antiques. I'm going to inherit the Silvine one day. What more can a man want?" Martin smiled his endearing smile.

What more indeed? But she didn't know whether he spoke the truth or not. On his own admission, he was a liar. "Are you going to tell your father you're not going into the hotel business, after all?"

"If you want me to give up the antiques, I will."

She caught her breath. "Give up that idea you told me about last night? About buying a place in the country?"

"If that's what you want."

He was too glib. She couldn't trust him. Again, she was aware of not getting straight answers. She thought, I don't need another reason to break off a wedding. One is enough. Stick to Antonia. She stood up. "There's nothing more to say. The wedding's off unless you promise to send Antonia home and not see her again."

Martin looked dreadfully hurt. "This could be the thin end of the wedge," he said. "How do I know you aren't going to get rid of all my friends, one by one?"

He was too wily for her. She couldn't think of clever answers. She was going to have to be blunt. "You must think I'm a fool," she said. "Let's forget Antonia. The reason the engagement is off is because you are a cheat. You intended, perhaps still intend, to cheat on your father, and you've cheated on me. Let's leave it at that." She put her free hand in her pocket, took out the sapphire ring he had given her and handed it to him. When he did not take it she slid it into his breast pocket, then strode across the lounge, slipping in and out of the chairs, and dumped the

14

roses on the desk. "Find a vase and put these in," she said to the astonished desk clerk. "Stick it somewhere. Not in my office." She didn't know if Martin was still where she had left him, or if he had gone. She had to hurry. She had to get away before there was a touch on her shoulder and she was obliged to look agan on Martin's engaging smile. Without glancing to right or left she swung round, walked to the lift and stepped inside.

There were tears on her cheeks when she opened the outer door of the penthouse. She brushed them aside. Her father was emerging from his study, looking disturbed. He gave her a searching look.

"I've been on to Oliver," he said. "He and Elaine are not very pleased with Martin. They're going to have a talk with him, then they'll be in touch."

"And I've been talking to Martin. He came round with roses," she said stonily.

"Oh, good chap. He's sorry." Her father looked gravely relieved. "I'm sure you'll be able to settle your differences. Lovers' tiffs," he said, sounding indulgent and understanding. "And they're going to talk to that woman Antonia."

"It sounds as though they know her well."

Her father seemed to think her remark could be ignored. "Did you tell them Martin had brought her over here?"

"They know she's here. I told them. It doesn't follow, Julie, that he brought her here."

"Oh no. She nipped over to try out the Eurotunnel. People do. And Martin just happened to discover she was here."

Her father ignored the sarcasm. "They'll be here this afternoon," he said.

"And Martin doesn't know they're coming?"

"I dare say they know how to get hold of him."

"I dare say they do," she retorted. "Well, I'd like to make it clear I don't intend to see Martin's parents. I don't want to and I haven't the time. And talking about knowing people well, I've discovered I didn't know Martin at all. I must have been led astray because of the fact that we come from such similar backgrounds. He fitted

15

in. I've learned you can be in love with someone without knowing them."

"Can you?" asked her father. He stood very straight in his military way, looking down at her. She could see he was holding his feelings in check. "I am beginning to think I don't know you, my own daughter."

"I'm sorry. I'm sorry you're so disappointed." She held on to her anger. She felt distanced from him. "I'm going to my office. I intend to cancel all the arrangements, then go away somewhere."

"Julie!" he came to life, protesting. "You can't go away."

"You were going to manage without me while I was on honeymoon," she retorted. "I'm only jumping ahead a bit."

"You can't simply walk out on the job and leave us flat."

No. She saw that, now. "All right," she said, "I'll cancel the wedding arrangements, then tie things up, then go."

"Julie, you cannot cancel the wedding at this late stage."

She hardened her heart. "As a matter of fact, I can."

"Think of the disruption—"

"Think of the disruption to my life if I went ahead so as not to disappoint the guests, then had to get a divorce."

She left him standing in the middle of the room, looking angry and bewildered, went out into the passage, glanced at the lift, then chose to walk down the stairs. There was something seriously bothering her. Lying awake in the night she had gone over and over the altercation with her parents. She remembered the flash of panic in her mother's eyes, swiftly hidden, when she had first announced she was not going to marry Martin. She had tried to come to terms with the fact that she had not been shown Antonia's letter. She had failed.

She thought about the fact that Oliver Wingate and his wife Elaine were as different from her own parents as chalk is from cheese. Wingate was striving, ruthless, carrying a chip on his shoulder from his early days. He had made no secret of the fact that he had been brought up in near-poverty. He was self-educated and shrewd. All he and her own father had in common was the hotel business. They were only the most casual of acquaintances until their children came

16

together. Until they brought their children together, she corrected herself, and once more felt that touch of alarm.

She wondered if Wingate wanted this amalgamation in order to move into a different kind of world. Might having his Hotel Silvine, an angular monster of the 20th century, amalgamated with the prestigious Hôtel le Sceptre in Paris, Le Bosquet in Geneva and the Merrion, one of the older and more dignified London hotels, appear to him to be a feather in his cap? What did her father want of it? He was older. Might he conceivably wish to opt out and take life more easily? She thought that was a possibility. He might think she was too young to be saddled with all the responsibility for three hotels. And that's true, she thought. I am certainly not ready. But if she was so important in his scheme of things why had he not taken her into his confidence when the matter of the amalgamation had been broached?

She crossed the foyer swiftly, went into her office, shut the door, turned on her computer and composed a letter to be sent to the guests advising them that the wedding was off. She added a note for her secretary, Melusine, telling her to start wrapping up the presents. Flowers. She rang the florist, fended off exclamations of surprise and dismay, then turned her attention to rearrangements within the hotel. Thank heavens the reception was to have been held here. She merely had to make arrangements for re-booking the rooms and cancelling the catering. The honeymoon hotel in the Caribbean was not her problem. Martin had done the bookings. When lunchtime came she had a sandwich sent in.

It was the middle of the afternoon when Georges, the elderly commissionaire tapped on the door and came in to say that the Wingates had arrived. "Your father has taken them up to the penthouse. He wants you."

"Thanks, Georges. But I'm going out," she said. "I'd be glad if you would give me five minutes then get a taxi."

"If there's anything I can do . . ." He waited expectantly.

She gave him a tight little smile. He was an old friend, had known her since she was a little girl. "You may have gathered the wedding's off."

17

He nodded. "I wondered. Monsieur and Madame Wingate looked upset. And your father." He waited again, forehead puckered.

"I guess they don't accept it's off, but it is, Georges. And I am about to run away. Don't worry about discretion. Everyone has to know. Send Pierre in, will you? See you in five minutes."

The door opened again and the deputy manager appeared. Julie placed a calm expression on her face. "Just in case the staff haven't got the drift of what's going on, you can tell them the wedding is off, Pierre."

He said, "I'm sorry, Mlle."

"Yes, well, so am I." She rose, reached for her jacket which was hanging on the wall and said, "If anyone asks for me tell them not to wait. I won't be back until quite late."

"Don't you think you ought to tell someone where you are?"

She hesitated. "I really don't want anyone coming after me."

"In case of real trouble, Julie."

"How very responsible of you, Pierre," she said as she slid the jacket round her shoulders. "All right. But remember I trust you. I'm going to Moira Ferroni's to see what I can sort out about the wedding dress, and then I'm going to look for somewhere to hide." She smiled at him.

"*Bien.*"

She went to the door then turned. "There's one thing I'm grateful for, Pierre. The loyalty of the staff."

The telephone rang. With one eye on the door she picked up the receiver. "Julie, the Wingates are here."

"I'm busy, Father."

"Julie."

"Martin's and my break-up is between him and me. I won't talk to his parents about it."

"They're going to get Martin over here."

"I told you. I've already seen him this morning."

"Julie. There are things to talk about."

"If you're referring to business, I haven't been consulted

about the amalgamation. It's too late now. I'm sorry, Father, but I'm going out." She put the receiver down.

Georges was holding open the door of a taxi. She smiled at him and gave the driver the address.

Moira's salon was in one of the grey stone buildings in the Avenue de la Grande Armée. Julie pushed the glass door open and went in. Moira was there talking to a client, looking the epitome of a smart *vendeuse* in a form-fitting black sheath of a dress and high heels. She had wide-apart dark eyes and a pointed chin. Her black hair was drawn severely away from her pussycat face so that she had the look of a ballet dancer. And she had a dancer's grace. She excused herself and came forward holding out her arms. "You have come for the dress, *cherie!*"

Julie looked wry. "I've come to talk to you about the dress. Can we go somewhere we won't be disturbed?"

"So." Moira spoke to her assistant and signed to Julie to follow her up a small flight of stairs that led to the room where clients tried on their prospective purchases. There was a standing triple mirror and huge windows looking into a small courtyard. She signed to Julie to sit down in a little gold painted chair and she sat down opposite. "Don't tell me the wedding's off? I can tell by your expression that something is very wrong."

Julie nodded and told her what had happened. Moira had put so much into the dress, a magnificent cream taffeta decorated with Brussells lace, that she felt nothing less than a full explanation was due. An assistant brought them coffee then went quietly out again. When Julie finished Moira said with a dismissive gesture of the hand, "The dress, forget it for the moment. It's advice you've come for—"

"No," Julie broke in edgily. "I don't need advice. I've made my decision, for better or worse. I just want to sort out the dress situation then I'm going down the street to make a booking. I have to get away and hide until this thing blows over."

"Where are you going?"

"I've no idea."

19

"I have a villa, the Villa Rosa, at Positano which I like my friends to use. No one would find you there."

Julie looked at her with wide-open, surprised eyes, for Moira was little more than an acquaintance. Scarcely a friend. She had made several outfits for Julie, and now the wedding dress.

"Don't you let it?"

"I like my friends to use it," Moira repeated. "You may go there if that is what you would like. You would have to fly to Naples and hire a car."

"I'd love it," breathed Julie.

"A good place for licking wounds," Moira said. "Now pick up that telephone over there and see if you can get a flight."

She was sorely tempted. She looked at the phone then looked away. "Yes," she said. "Yes, I will. Just as soon as I can manage it, that's where I will go."

Chapter Two

The brakes squeaked complainingly and the tyres swished on the gravel. Julie's breath caught in apprehension as she ran her hired car down the steep drive.

She could see the car-port on the roof of the villa fifty metres below the road. She flicked the mane of hair back from her face, put the little car into low gear, then crawled forward at a snail's pace on to the flat concrete that was the parking area as well as the villa's roof. She switched off the engine and slipped out swiftly and thankfully. Then she stood, entranced.

The Gulf of Salerno was spread before her. Away in the distance, far out to sea, hovered a great misty blue lion of a rock. "Capri!" She went to the balcony and leant over, drinking in the beauty. The pretty vine-hung villa clung like a butterfly to the rock cliff, with a stony garden, full of green and spiky cactus sweeping down to the sea.

The drive along the tortuously winding road that connected up the little towns and villages on the rocky coast had been a challenging one and Julie was tired. Swinging round, she picked up her suitcase, unlocked the door with the key Moira had given her, and struggled down the marble staircase into the heart of the villa. Here was a spacious hall and, looking round, she saw that rooms opened off it.

'There are four bedrooms,' Moira had said. 'Take the big one in the front. That one has the best view.'

Right. There it was. The door was open. She went in, put down her case and inspected the room with interest and pleasure. There was an enormous window with a view out to sea and another facing the cliff at the side.

The room was intriguingly furnished with an enormous

baroque bed, covered with hand-crocheted lace, a Chinese screen, an antique dressing table and a scatter of fluffy rugs.

Julie glanced uncertainly at herself in a long mirror, then turned away sharply. Her face was pale, her blue eyes reddened still from crying. She didn't want to think about what had happened at the hotel this morning. The slim, cinnamon-coloured dress in which she had made her precipitous departure from Paris was now limp with the heat, her hair untidy, drooping round her ears, damply clinging to her neck. There was a ladder in her tights and her lipstick, the only makeup she wore normally, had long gone. She kicked off her strappy shoes and went to explore the rest of the building.

The salon was a big, sunny room personalised with heavily carved antiques, a host of bright cushions and fluffy rugs. A lively, lived-in room, expensive like Moira's salon, yet a room to be at home in. There was a glass-topped coffee-table, useful and beautiful, some colourful ceramic ashtrays, an enormous arrangement of dried flowers, a number of well-painted local scenes showing the towering cliffs, the lively sea.

The dining-room was small and elegant, with pretty painted chairs and another glass-topped table. And next door, in a cook's dream of a kitchen, bright orange saucepans hung like marigolds from pegs on the wall.

Beyond the hall was an outer door. Investigation proved it opened on to the steep rocky garden ablaze with geraniums and green with spiky cactus. A narrow path danced downwards towards the sea. On the opposite side of the hall another door opened on to a balcony, half-sunlit, half-shaded by a blaze of pink and purple bougainvillaea.

'It's the ideal place in which to nurse your bruises,' Moira had said, 'and restore your torn self-esteem.' Julie warmly agreed.

She leaned her elbows on the balcony rail, listening to the sea, the cry of a gull, the rustle of a leaf in the bougainvillaea as a feather of breeze crept in. For the first time in days, she felt a sense of calm, a tentative peace, creep over her.

The merest movement on the rocks below caught her eye. Julie stared, blinked. A man was coming round a spur, looking up. But this garden, this cliff, was supposed to be impregnable! No one, Moira had said, could get in except through the door on the roof, or from the sea. Julie watched with apprehension as he made his way up towards the villa. He wore swimming trunks and as he came closer she saw his feet were bare.

She spun round and went with quick, nervous footsteps into the hall. A moment later the bell rang but before she could reach it the door burst open.

The man who stood before her was deeply tanned and his black hair, roughened from immersion in the sea, fell carelessly across a high forehead. He looked her up and down, as though he owned the place and it was she who trespassed. "I wondered where the key was," he said. "I must say I was not expecting you. I thought I was destined to stay outside for ever." He had sea-green eyes, startling in the dark face, and a well-cut but hard mouth. His high-bridged Roman nose gave him an arrogant air. There was an underlying toughness about him, a confidence that splintered Julie's new-found sense of security.

What could she say? "How did you get into the garden?" she asked.

"Oh," he replied, "that wasn't difficult."

"The villa has been loaned to me," she said, hoping her nervousness didn't show. "What are you doing here?"

"OK," he replied laconically, "we'll have to work this out. I'll go and get my bag. I've tucked it into a rock. The key was not where Moira normally keeps it, so I had a swim. Then I saw the car on the roof!" He smiled. "I'll be back in a minute."

Julie stood on the step watching him as he went down the steep rock stairway that must lead to the bottom of the garden and the sea. What on earth was she going to do? Was he genuine? Certainly he knew Moira's name. And there was no doubt, unless he was a superb actor, he

23

had been here before. He had walked into the villa without looking around, without either surprise or interest in his surroundings. But then, wouldn't any professional burglar or confidence trickster behave like that?

'I like my friends to use the villa,' Moira had said. Maybe he had a standing invitation. But if so, why had she not been warned? She reminded herself that she didn't know Moira very well. At least not in a personal way. Their contact was solely through Julie's clothes. Moira had not visited Le Septre. Julie had not been to her home. But then, one could be on intimate terms with the French for years without ever being invited to their homes. She recognised that she was being unfair. Had Moira, feeling sorry for her, not wanting her to be alone, set this up? Had she perhaps even decided that a little *affaire* on the rebound was the route to Julie's recovery? I've got manipulation on the brain, she said to herself, ruefully.

But what was she going to do now? There was no telephone with which to ring Moira in Paris.

The man had disappeared from sight round a jutting rock. She wandered back inside and went to one of the big windows that looked out on the sea. She seemed to be there for a long time. Maybe, she thought with a mixture of optimism and fear, he won't come back. Maybe he has taken to his heels. That would be a relief. She thought she would give him a few minutes then lock the door. A voice called from the hall, "So here I am."

She swung round. He was putting his bag down on the floor. He came to join her at the window. She looked up at him. "This is very awkward," she said. "Moira told me the villa would be empty."

He stood with feet apart looking at her consideringly, hands on hips. "She told me that, too. Still—" his hard mouth flicked up at the edges. "If I have to share I couldn't have chosen my companion better myself."

"There has obviously been some mistake," she said, ignoring his flattery. "One of us will have to go."

He raised one eyebrow, inclining his head as though admitting she had a point, yet at the same time questioning

24

it. He said, "The last bus has gone. There isn't another until morning."

"You haven't got a car?"

"No."

"I'll run you back," she offered tentatively. "To Amalfi, or anywhere else where you might find accommodation. Maybe in Positano, even."

"Not at this time of year," he replied.

He leaned back, hands lightly on his hips. He seemed to grow taller as he looked at her. Though the green eyes were veiled, the mouth still, she had a very certain and rather frightening feeling that he was laughing.

"OK. You don't mind if I get my things and change into respectable travelling gear in one of the bedrooms, do you?"

"No, of course not." She could not believe he had given in so easily. She watched him as he went with long strides down the hall. So he did know his way around the villa. Or was he making a guess? It would not be difficult. She swung round and went back to her room. Lifting her bag on to the bed, she began to unpack.

Footsteps sounded in the hall. Julie grabbed the car keys, slipped into a pair of flat-heeled shoes and hurried out. He watched her as she approached. Now he wore designer jeans and – heavens – a silk shirt. A silk shirt and no car!

As though he read something in her expression, he said, "It's a pity to have to part without even introducing ourselves."

And it was. She was being edgy. Perhaps rude. He was being incredibly good-natured. She said, "I'm Julie Creighton."

"Greg Strathallan."

"How do you do?" They both laughed, he with zest and warmth, she somewhat nervously.

"It's really very good of you to be so co-operative," she said. He acknowledged her compliment with a nod, his eyes twinkling.

"I – er – I've got a bottle of duty-free gin," she went on. "Can I give you a drink before you go?" she added quickly, "It's the least I can do in view of – in view of—"

"Sure," he replied. "My co-operativeness?" Those eyes really danced now.

He swung round and with a jaunty step headed towards the kitchen. She went to her room and returned with the gin.

He already had two glasses on the worktop and was dropping ice cubes into them. He glanced up with a smile.

"A very small measure for me, please. And a lot of tonic," Julie said, handing him the bottle.

"Right."

She found herself smiling at him in return. There was a darting, dancing warmth in him that seemed to encircle her, then shoot away. "You appear to know your way about?" she said, making the statement sound like a question.

"I've stayed here many times. Moira's an old friend."

"Really?"

"Yes, really. Here's your drink." She took it from him. "Cheers," he said. "If it's not a rude question, what are you doing here – you and a bottle of gin?"

She found herself laughing. He was good company. "I ran into Moira in Paris. She insisted I come here. I – er – needed a break."

"I see. Let's take our drinks on to the balcony, shall we? The sea's beautiful at this time with the sun going down over Capri." He put his glass down and carried a cushioned, wrought iron chair out through the glass door.

Julie followed suit. Since her violent exit from the hotel this morning, a departure she would rather not think about, Julie had spoken to no one except the airline staff and the car hire man. She was suddenly glad of even such dubious company as this man provided.

The sun was going down in a blaze of scarlet and gold. Greg held up the glass to the light. "So how do you happen to be on your own, a pretty girl like you? There has to be a reason."

"Not really," she said evasively. "I was tired. I've been awfully busy. I needed a break."

"So you cut yourself off from all your friends and

26

acquaintances?" He looked quizzical. She did not answer. There was a long silence. She tried to put the conversation back on its feet and failed. There were a bad few moments.

He drained his glass. "Let's go, shall we? Thanks for the drink."

Yes. He must go. At the foot of the marble staircase he picked up his bag. They climbed the stairs together, went out on to the roof. Greg put his bag in the boot, held the door open for her, then slid into the passenger seat. Julie switched on the ignition and pressed the starter.

Nothing. The engine was dead. She pressed the starter once again; there was no response.

"The battery's flat," said Strathallan complacently.

"But how can it be flat?" Her voice rose. "I've driven all the way from Naples airport today. Even if the battery was running down when I took the car, it would have recharged itself on the way here."

He shrugged. They sat in silence for a moment, then, hopelessly, she pressed the starter again. "Do you know anything about engines?"

"Not a thing," he replied. Then added with a twinkle, "Horses, now. Ask me anything at all about horses and I'll tell you." He drummed his fingers on the metal body work. "But engines, no, I'm afraid not. This isn't a very promising start to your holiday," he commented and grinned.

Her blue eyes met his. Panic swept over her. "What have you done to the car?"

He pretended to be offended. "What a suspicious young woman you are. Do I look like the kind of person who would disconnect a girl's battery?"

She wanted to say, 'Yes, you do. Besides, you had time to slip up here.' But she did not want to be contentious. Play it cool. For heaven's sake, play it cool.

"I'd ring the police for you," he said helpfully, "but there's no telephone. Moira doesn't want to be bothered with calls when she's down here. Well, that's that, I suppose." He opened the door, stepped out and manhandled his bag from the boot. "You appear to be stuck with me," he remarked cheerfully. "Not that I mind sharing a beautiful villa with a beautiful girl."

He looked such a picture of confidence that she burst out: "You did mess around with the car, didn't you? I know you did!"

"What bad characters you associate with," he replied but the words were so gentle, so amused, so lacking in offence that the fear went. And then he chuckled softly and she knew he was guilty and, mischievously, he did not care that she knew.

She slid her key in the lock and pushed the heavy wooden door open. Greg was behind her. For a moment she was tempted to slam the door in his face but she didn't. She went on down the stairs leaving him to follow. At least there was a key to her room so she could lock herself in. She went inside and did just that.

It didn't take long to unpack her bag. She looked at her watch. Six o'clock. She stretched out on the bed. Perhaps if she gave him time he would take himself off. Exhausted from the events of the day, she drifted into a troubled sleep.

When she awakened, the room was in darkness. She rubbed her eyes, turned on the light, looked at her watch. Eight o'clock! The villa was silent. Out at sea, a motorboat scudded by. Had her unwelcome guest departed? In the beautiful, green-tiled bathroom with its gold taps and fluffy gold rugs she showered swiftly, pulled on a pair of silk trousers and then, defiantly, the very special Italian blouse that had been part of her trousseau.

Moira had told her of a good restaurant about one kilometre along the road and farther up the mountainside. Carefully, she unlocked the door, pushed it open a fraction, then angrily shoved it wide. But the anger lasted only a moment. He was standing in the doorway to the salon, a glass in his hand. That soft lock of dark hair had fallen over his forehead again and his shirt was open at the neck.

"I hope you enjoyed your siesta." He looked her over

carefully, taking in every detail of her dress. "Good. You're all ready to go," he said, just as though he had agreed to wait. "I was beginning to get mighty peckish. There's an excellent restaurant up the hill where the service is good and the food superb." He smiled down at her with engaging charm.

"I – I—" she began.

He strode down the length of the hall, took her arm and moved her towards the little staircase that led up to the roof.

"Oh hell!" To her dismay, Julie found herself going with him.

They walked down the steep and winding road that led from the Villa Rosa into the little town. They could see it below them, a cluster of golden lights, thick by the shore, thinning out as they went into the mountain. Greg was tall and he had a long stride. Julie adjusted hers. He took her arm.

"We cross here and climb some steps." They waited for a little line of cars to pass then hurried across the road. The steps were hewn out of the granite mountainside. They were not particularly steep, and there were lights to guide them.

The restaurant clung to the hillside as did all the buildings on this precipitous coastline. On either side of the steps that wound their way up through the garden were sweet-smelling flowers and shrubs dotted with coloured lights. They turned and looked back on the town. "It's beautiful," breathed Julie. She felt softened by the beauty of the scene. High above them a powdery white lane spread itself across the sky. The Milky Way. Outside it, in the velvet darkness, stars twinkled and shone. Greg slid an arm through hers, turned her round. "We're nearly there."

They crossed a stretch of dry grass. To the left there were big arched windows through which they glimpsed people sitting at white clothed tables. This building must have once been a monastery. Ahead, stone-flagged cloisters and within them groups of diners at little tables. Bright table cloths. More tables spilled out on to the grass. Julie swung round. From where they stood now, at the side of the restaurant, there was a magnificent view across to the next headland.

"Can we sit out here? It's perfect." She felt she had never been in so romantic a place. She felt enfolded in its beauty and its magic.

"Why not?" Greg seemed softened, too.

A waiter in a white coat came hurrying from the door that led off the cloisters into the restaurant. He greeted Greg like an old friend. *"Buon giorno."*

Greg replied in fluent Italian.

The young man smiled and bowed to Julie, then showed them to a table for two beneath a blaze of bright pink bougainvillaea.

He held out a chair for her, spoke to her in Italian, then, smiling, went away. "What was he saying?"

"Something nice."

Almost immediately he returned with a hibiscus flower which he presented to Julie with a little bow.

Puzzled, she turned to Greg. "Why did he give me this?"

"I told him we're here for a very special celebration. You know Italians. They love a bit of romance."

She pushed her chair back but he reached across the table and took her wrist.

"Relax," he said, then added gently, "Have fun, Julie. I do read the gossip columns, you know. There's only one way to get out of despair. Kill it, celebrate its demise, and move on. Sitting round an empty villa all by yourself isn't a cure for anything."

"Did Moira send you?"

He raised one eyebrow and when she repeated the question, ignored it. "There's champagne coming. It's time to start having fun. Italians are good at this sort of thing. At fun, and loving, and friendship."

He glanced aside. The other tables were filled with glamorously dressed diners. There were Italian women in bright silks that set off their olive skins and shining black hair, a spattering of tourists and two or three families: the old grandmother, a teenager or two, some toddlers staying

30

up late in the Italian way. Two women, both in their twenties, both elegantly turned out in silk and wearing masses of heavy gold jewellery, sauntered down from the terrace. They eyed Julie curiously. Greg raised a hand to them, casually.

What was she going to do now? Julie wondered nervously. She had been a fool to give in and come here. But no doubt she would feel better able to cope with him on a full stomach.

She smiled, tremulously.

"That's better," Greg said as a waiter approached. "Now, what are we going to order? *Insalata di mare?*"

Julie loved the little salads of prawns and squid that she had tasted on previous Italian coastal holidays. She nodded. "I'd like that."

"And to follow? How would you like veal with artichokes, mushrooms and stuffed baby marrows?" She nodded again. The waiter had gone. Greg leaned towards her. "What, may I ask, have you eaten today?"

"Er . . ." Her voice tailed off.

"Yes, I thought so." He added with surprising gentleness, "It's very important to eat."

"Yes. Yes, of course." Then, in an effort to steer the conversation away from herself, "You speak Italian very well."

"I was a year at the University of Rome. My father happened to be doing a considerable amount of business here at the time. In the end I didn't join him, but the study has paid off."

She raised dark-lashed, querying eyes.

"What do you do?"

"I work in the City."

"London?"

"Of course. Where else? But we didn't come here to talk about me. You've got a problem." There must have been something in her expression that touched him, for his face softened and he covered her hand where it lay on the table. "Do you want to tell me about it?"

Her nerves jumped. She felt if she talked about what Martin

31

had done she might break down. "You already seem to be pretty well informed," she said shortly, and immediately wished she had been able to use a softer tone. Somehow her emotions had taken over her voice.

"I know that one Miss Julie Creighton was to marry one Mr Martin Whatsit," he said deliberately.

Whatsit! She looked up sharply, but his expression was bland.

"Quite a fanfare of trumpets there were to have been too," he went on. "A very suitable match, the columnists said." He leaned towards her and she felt herself stiffening, drawing back. "I'm only suggesting that if it would help to tell me why the bride has found her way to southern Italy alone—"

"It's really none of your business." This time, though she broke in on him she did speak gently and even managed a stiff little smile.

"Of course. It's nobody's business but your own. And yet," Greg added realistically, "sometimes an outsider can help. I don't like to see any girl unhappy."

"I really don't think it would help to talk," she said. "I don't know who you are or anything about you. I—"

"Here's the champagne," he broke in as though she had not spoken. The waiter put an ice bucket down on the table and proceeded, smilingly, to ease out the cork and fill Julie's glass.

She raised it to her lips. "Here's to a happy holiday," she said stiffly. "I'm sorry about the muddle. Tomorrow I'll have someone look at the car, and then I'll drive you to a hotel."

"The car's all right again."

She put the glass down with a bump, splashing some of it on the table-top.

"What do you mean?"

He smiled back at her, benign, innocent. "I tried the engine while you were asleep. You left the keys. It's going perfectly."

The waiter came and served their first course.

"I'd have told you before that the car is OK but I didn't

32

want you rushing me off and missing your dinner," Greg said when the man had gone. "Raise your glass, Julie. Come on," he added as she sat mutely not knowing what to do, again feeling trapped. "Raise your glass," he repeated softly but with such authority that somehow, without quite realising she was obeying him, Julie found herself doing just that.

They had nearly finished their fish salad when there was a scraping of chairs and the two women left their table. Julie watched as they wended their way between the diners and disappeared into the restaurant building. Faintly giddy from the effect of the champagne on an empty stomach, she thought, 'I'll go after them.'

The champagne made her brave. She snatched her handbag. "Excuse me a moment."

He rose. His manners were exemplary. She hurriedly crossed the courtyard, threaded her way between the little tables and followed the direction taken by the two women. She stepped up on to a veranda where there was the powder-room sign. She paused outside, her fingers on the gilt handle. The door stood ajar and she could hear their laughter. A voice said, in French, "Isn't the girl always the same type? Long fair hair, long legs, neat features. Looks right in his sports car with the wind in her face. Or at the prow of the yacht in a bikini."

"He stamps them out with a paper pattern cutter," said another voice and they laughed unkindly. "No doubt we'll see her on *Neptuna* tomorrow. I wonder where he got her."

"And what he's going to do with her. Isn't that more to the point?" There was a low laugh.

Julie let go of the handle. Why should those people be talking about her? she asked herself feverishly. Plenty of girls had long blonde hair, long legs and neat features. 'Go and ask them. Go on,' she urged herself. But she could not. Her nerve had gone. Then the other voice said, "The police have been asking questions again. I wonder if she knows."

Her nerves jumped. Knows what?

At the far end of the passage, just off the veranda, Julie could see a small office. There was a thin clerk with olive

33

skin and shining black hair seated behind a glass partition. She ran towards him. "Signora?"

"Do you speak English?" she asked him breathlessly.

"A leetle. Is something wrong?"

"Is it possible to telephone Paris from here?"

"It is possible, signora, but there is the question of cost."

"You can find out from the exchange what it costs, and I will pay." The man's face closed. She tried not to panic. "I'm dining here with Mr Greg Strathallan. I'm sure you know him?" A moment of breathless anticipation while she waited for his answer.

He shook his head. "Strathallan. I do not know."

Her heart sank. "Please let me use the phone. Look, here's the number." She put her notebook down on the desk in front of him. "Please, it's important. Look, here's the money in advance." She produced several thousand lire from her bag. His face brightened a little, then, still with reluctance, he began to dial. She could tell by his absorbed face that he was through and was listening to the distant ringing at the other end. She cast an apprehensive look behind, half-expecting that Greg had come looking for her.

"Is no reply," said the clerk at last. "I think there is no one at home."

"There will be an answer machine. I can leave a message.

He shook his head. "No answer machine."

She turned away. "Thank you. *Gracias*."

"You were away a long time," Greg said when she returned to the table. "Are you all right? I had to send the waiter away with the veal."

She smiled apologetically. "Sorry." He eyed her enigmatically as he signed to the waiter to return. She sat down, feeling defeated. There was silence between them. "I was trying to ring Moira," she said at last.

"How very sensible of you," he said. "Now here's the veal. Doesn't it look delicious? Let me top up your glass."

She sipped her drink, looking at him through narrowed eyes. She drew a deep breath, right up from the bottom of

34

her lungs, gathered her courage and said boldly, "Are you involved with the police?"

"No."

She picked up her fork, then put it down again. "It strikes me as odd," she said, "that you don't say, 'Why should you ask?'"

He smiled that enigmatic smile. "I assume you have your reasons and if you want to tell me, you will."

She had never met anyone who was so sure of himself. She wanted to ask him if he owned a yacht called *Neptuna*. Was a man without a car likely to own a yacht? She must have misheard. They must have been talking about someone else. It was pure chance that the description fitted. Long legs. Long hair. After all, they hadn't mentioned his name. She thought, I am being silly. Panicky. He's a friend of Moira's.

But she didn't know Moira very well.

"Aren't you going to eat your dinner?"

"I'm thinking," she said.

"I know. If I could see into your brain I'm sure I would see wheels whirling round and round."

She found herself laughing. "Look," she said, "you can stay at the villa. I'm going to find a room somewhere."

"Finish your meal first," Greg said kindly.

She blinked, pushed the soft hair back from her face. Could the problem be solved as easily as that? "But – do you know of a—"

"Any waiter will be glad to help you. They've all got a grandmother or aunt or cousin who lets the best bedroom for a modest sum."

She smiled at him gratefully and he smiled back. She picked up her fork. The food was delicious.

Now that the problem was solved she chatted more easily. Greg knew the coast well. He had been here many times. He told her he worked in the City of London. "When I get too stressed I take off and come here," he said. He told her the name of the company he worked for. Julie did not know it. But why should I doubt his word? she asked herself. I don't know the names of all the financial companies in the City. The champagne was taking effect. She decided she had been panicky, and foolish. Why shouldn't she be friends with him? All right, they had got off to a bad start, but not that bad. She would telephone Moira tomorrow and sort the situation out. Meantime . . .

"My," said Greg leaning across the table, holding up his glass, "how those wheels whirr!"

She couldn't help laughing. "All right. I'll relax."

The waiter came with the menu. "I can recommend the sweets," Greg said so she ordered ice-cream which came packed with fruit and nuts. They sat drinking strong black coffee and looking past the fairy-lights on the edge of the cloisters to stars that glittered in an ink-dark sky. He told her about Positano. How it had been founded by the inhabitants of Paestum when their own homes were sacked by invaders. How it had later been ruled by a Benedictine Abbey until the inhabitants rebelled. He told her scandalous stories about the nobles who had taken it over, Alfonso il Magnanimo and the Marquis of Oliveto.

It was a magical evening. When Greg called for the bill she was loath to go. She sat dreaming while he found his credit card, watching him, waiting for him to ask the waiter about a room for her, regretting they had to part.

"Come on," he said placing the tip on a plate. "Let's go." He touched her arm and she felt a charge go through her, quite wonderful, and mysterious. A haunting tenderness.

She rose, and spoke reluctantly. "I have to ask about that room."

He brushed the matter carelessly aside. "You won't be happy leaving me alone in the villa. I understand that you feel it's your responsibility. I'll be on my way."

She recognised that she ought to be breathing a sigh of relief. Instead she asked, "Where will you go?"

He shrugged. "I'll be all right."

But would he? He had no car. Why did he not have a car? How had he got here? Why had she not asked him that? Had he come by bus? He didn't seem the kind of man who would travel by bus. "You haven't got a car." There, it was out. Her greatest suspicion.

36

"No," he said, "that's true. But there are other means of transport."

"You can be provocative, can't you?"

"Do you call it provocative to travel by plane, bus, taxi or boat?"

There was no answer to that. They walked down the steps together, Greg solicitously holding her arm. They paused to survey the golden lights of the town. "Isn't it beautiful!" she breathed. The moon had risen, lifting the darkness from the sea. The Milky Way was a magnificent path of stars stretching across the sky. She gazed around her, enchanted. Greg's arm was through hers. It was warm and comforting.

She thought, this is a ridiculous situation and I am behaving like a nineteenth century spinster. Why shouldn't he stay at the Villa Rosa? Anyway, I have a key to my room. And he's a friend of Moira's. What would Moira say when she told her that in spite of Greg's insistence that he was a friend she had thrown him out? Her thoughts reverted to the two gossipy women she had overheard in the powder-room. Maybe they hadn't been talking about Greg? Maybe she had misheard. Maybe they had been talking about him at first but when they mentioned the police they had switched to someone else. He had been so cool when she mentioned the police.

"How those wheels spin!" he said again.

She looked up into his face, lit by moonlight, and saw laughter in the curve of his lips, the shining eyes. She said impulsively, "Of course you must stay at the villa."

"Of course," he agreed and they laughed together, softly, companionably.

They said goodnight in the hall and Julie went to her room, closed the door and went to turn the key. It was not there. For a moment she stared blankly at the keyhole, then a shiver of sheer terror passed through her and she realised what a thin film of trust she had laid over this man. She flung the door open and strode across the hall. His bedroom door was open. He was not there. She swung round and there he was standing on the balcony watching her, smoking a cigarette with his back to the sea. His face was shadowed so that she could not see his expression.

"Give me back my key," she demanded. "How dare you take it away!"

He came towards her, walking slowly and deliberately, the cigarette held aside in his hand, glowing. "Because you don't trust me, Miss Julie Creighton. That's why. I cannot share a villa with someone who doesn't trust me."

"How can I trust a man who puts my car out of commission so that he can spend the night with me?" she demanded furiously.

"You flatter yourself," he said icily. "I don't have to take another man's fiancée. And such a man! Martin Wingate! I was at school with him. I knew him well. I knew you were in distress, probably not capable of getting yourself from A to B if I read you correctly, and if you were my worst enemy I wouldn't stand aside at such a time. So the engagement's off! I congratulate you. If ever there was a two-timing creep it's Martin Wingate. We crossed swords at school and I've given him a wide berth since. I can't imagine what your father's up to."

"It's nothing to do with—"

"Isn't it?" he asked sardonically. "You don't do yourself much of a favour." Before she could reply he began again, "I put your car out of commission so that I could take you out to dinner, introduce you to something you needed badly, a bit of relaxation. What were you going to do here alone in the villa? Mull? Weep? Jump out the window? I was worried about you."

She could only stare at him. And then the tears of humiliation and despair began to run down her face. It was too soon to be found out. Too soon to be comforted. Too soon . . . She swung round, strode to her room.

Chapter Three

Sleep eluded her. Tossing and turning hour after hour in a room flooded with moonlight, listening to the murmur of the sea below, wrestling with her thoughts, Julie had never felt more alone. Or more foolish. She supposed it was inevitable that a hotel amalgamation would promote talk in the financial section of the City, but why should there be suppositions as to whether pressure had been put on the young people to marry? That, it seemed to her, was what Greg meant when he said he could not imagine what her father was up to. But she and Martin had been in love. She had never realised that their love affair had taken place in a goldfish bowl.

She began again to toss and turn. At last, when the little diamond watch on her wrist – her father's present, in gratitude, she wondered sardonically, for marrying Martin – said three, she rose. She put on the new négligé, white satin patterned with lovers' knots – they seemed ridiculous, now – and crept along to the kitchen. She would make herself a cup of tea.

A shaft of moonlight from the big window showed Greg's bedroom door wide open. But of course he would be fast asleep. She went on, her feet soundless on the cool tiles. As she came abreast of the door, she paused, blinking in disbelief. The bed had not been slept in. His suitcase had gone.

She flashed round, went from one room to another. They were all empty. At a loss, she stood in the hall. What could Greg's disappearance mean? That he was, after all, a very plausible high class thief? That he had a van hidden away somewhere in these rocky clefts? She remembered with dismay the conversation she had overheard from the ladies' powder-room at the hotel. Why on earth had she not questioned him? And then she remembered that she had, but she had not gone far enough. When a man has taken you out to dinner good manners preclude your suggesting he might be some sort of a criminal. Oh hell!

Heart thudding, stiff with apprehension, she looked swiftly round the salon. Was anything missing? A Chinese porcelain figure. There it was. Pictures? She walked round the room examining the walls. There were no marks indicating that a picture might have been removed. There was a large vase, easily portable, on a shelf. She thought it was cloisonné and must be valuable. He had not taken that. She went to the drinks cabinet. Stacks of Waterford glass and no spaces where some pieces may have been removed.

She allowed herself a quick little sigh of relief then went to look in the dining-room. There was a Chinese carpet that must be valuable. And it was still here. She pulled out drawers in the sideboard. There was plenty of silver but at a glance she thought it wasn't valuable. And anyway, it was still there. She went into the bedrooms one after the other. But she scarcely knew what she was looking for. How long had she been in the villa when Greg arrived? Minutes? She thought she had had time for only a cursory glance around. There were small antiques on bedside tables. More pictures. Carpets.

She wondered about the fact that Moira allowed her friends free rein with a villa that contained such valuable furnishings. But then, if all her friends were rich, it could be assumed that this was what they would expect of a holiday villa. And come to think of it, it had not always been a holiday villa. She remembered Moira telling her only a few months ago that it had been her parents' home. That her father had died several years ago and her mother recently. That she wanted to keep the villa as it was, as a home.

Might Greg, she asked herself now, if he knew the villa well, have come for one specific and valuable object? If only there had been a telephone she could have rung Moira. Why had she not tried again last night after dinner? She knew why. Because she had been lulled by Greg's charm into a false sense of security. And the champagne. Fool! she said to herself. Fool!

Then she remembered he had been to school with Martin. But had he? She had only his word for that. Why had she not asked questions? Same answer, she said to herself. She had been distracted by his charm. And the champagne. How wise of him, she thought, to ply her, a tired woman with an empty stomach, with champagne. Then she remembered the gin she had felt impelled to offer him, and which she had drunk with him. I don't suppose that helped in keeping my wits about me, she thought, angry with herself.

She checked the front door. It was still locked and the key was inside. She opened it and looked out. Her hired car was there. She went back, re-locked the door and remembering that Greg had arrived from the garden, went to that door. It was, of course, unlocked. The steps leading down through the steep garden were dark. She went outside and looked up. The wall here was obscured by thick vine. Could he have climbed up there? Not without leaving torn plants, she decided. Might there be a ladder hidden away? She would have to look in the daylight. Even so, it did not make sense to climb out from here when he could easily enough use the front door.

Leaving it open, though. She thought about that. If she took him at face value she had to admit he was a considerate man. She locked the garden door and went back to bed. There was no alarm clock in any of the bedrooms. After all, she said to herself wryly, it is a holiday villa. She thumped the pillow eight times. Sometimes it worked.

She slid into bed and slept desultorily for some hours, then fell into a deep, dreamless sleep. When she wakened it was nearly nine o'clock. So much for the pillow-thumping. The room was flooded with light. She looked round, at the cool, pale green walls, the elegant beige curtains with their decorative green leaves, and wondered for a moment where she was. Then the events of the night before flooded into her mind. She leaped out of bed, flung her honeymoon wrap around her and went barefoot out into the hall. The villa was silent. Empty. She knew, unequivocally, that she was alone.

She went back into her room, slipped into a pair of jeans and a T-shirt, brushed her hair, then went to the kitchen and made herself a cup of coffee. The car keys were on the little table at the bottom of the short flight of stairs that led out on to the roof. She picked up her handbag, ran up the stairs to the outer door, locked it after her and jumped into the car.

Nine-thirty. Moira should be at the salon.

She was not. "Moira has gone to see a client," her assistant said, "and we do not know when she will be back."

"Ah-h-h!" What to do now? Julie wracked her brains. Moira often visited new clients at home. 'You cannot design for a woman if you do not know her,' she would say. The quickest way to sum up the personality of a stranger, Moira thought, was to see them in their own surroundings. It often meant that she was gone all day.

"Would you care to leave a message, M'selle?"

"Yes," said Julie, making up her mind. "Yes. Tell her Greg Strathallan is here and I need to know who he is. She had better telegraph me." She drove back up the winding road to the cliff-top villa feeling disturbed. Why did life have to be so frustrating? Then she looked to her right and there was the sea glimmering and glittering in the morning sunshine. Her spirits rose. She put her foot on the accelerator. Now for a swim. In the sun and sea she would forget her problems. She changed into her bikini, picked up a towel, let herself out of the back door and looked round for somewhere to hide the key. She slipped it in between two loose stones then started down the narrow steps. The path led across an outcrop of rock and on to another steep little flight on the cliff proper. Half-way down she paused, looking round. There was no sign of a path leading up out of the garden to the road. The buttressing was formidable. There would be no climbing up there. Or down either, for that matter.

Spiky cactus and little crusty wildflowers grew on either side of the steps. Here she had to duck her head to go through a small tunnel. It was a wild, fascinating garden. A dangerous garden if one did not step warily. Near the bottom there was a fringe of great boulders. She went between them and came out on a small beach.

The sun was hot, the water deliciously cool. She swam out with long, steady strokes, then turned over on her back, eyes closed against the glare of the sun. It would not take long to acquire a tan here, she thought. After a few moments she turned over again and swam lazily towards a high outcrop of rock that partially hid the little pier she had seen from her bedroom window.

There was a yacht idling at its moorings. It was a beautiful vessel, quite fifty feet long. There was a large flush deck aft, ideal for sunbathing. She swam right up to it, then trod water, blinking the salt from her eyes.

"*Neptuna*." She said the word out loud. "*Neptuna!*" That was the name being tossed about by the two women she had heard talking in the restaurant last night. They had been discussing some playboy . . . They had said he took out girls with long legs.

Her thoughts broke off leaving her seriously disquietened. Her gaze roved over the cliff, looking for paths, but even the one she had come down was obscured now by the prickly cactus and mountain plants. She saw the beach was hemmed in by rocks and the cliff at either end. There was no path, so how had Greg . . .

"Welcome aboard," said a familiar voice that came from high above her head. She spun round. The shock made her pause just a moment too long and she went under. She came up, gasping for air. He was leaning against the deckhouse. She shook the water out of her eyes.

"So you came looking for me," said Greg Strathallan, laughing. "I'm flattered."

She grasped the lowest rung of the yacht's metal ladder, looking up at him, angry with herself for not guessing.

"Come on up," he invited, smiling down at her.

"No thanks." She dived down through the clear green water, swimming beneath the surface until her lungs were bursting. When she surfaced, Greg was beside her. His hand shot out and he pushed her under again.

She dived away, surfaced, felt his hand on her head again, swung round and swam strongly away but when she surfaced he was there once more, hand raised, laughing.

"Pax," she cried, laughing with him now, gasping.

"Are you coming aboard?"

"Yes. Yes."

"Race you, then."

He beat her to the ladder by several yards.

She grasped the lowest rung and climbed lithely up, then slid over the rail on to the deck. Greg came swiftly after her. "You swim very well," he said.

"Nearly as well as you." She squeezed the water out of her hair. "So you didn't sleep at the villa."

"I knew you were safe. And I like the stars for company. Have you ever slept on deck and watched the sun rise?"

"Actually, no. What a lovely yacht! Whose is it?"

He leaned back against the railing, laughing. "I stole it from the marina at Fiumincino. Don't you think I've got good taste?"

"Very." His laughter was infectious. "If you've discovered where the towels are kept, I'd like to give my hair a rub."

"I'll try and find one." He disappeared down the companionway and a moment later a bright red towel came flying up. Julie gave her hair a quick rub, then tied it into a turban.

"That's very fetching," Greg remarked approvingly, emerging on deck again. "Would you like to see over *Neptuna*? Oh, by the way, have you had any breakfast?" When she shook her head he added, "I'll put the coffee on. Follow me."

It was indeed a luxurious craft. The saloon was carpeted in clipped sheepskin, the walls panelled in light oak. There was a cocktail cabinet in one corner, discreetly masquerading as a cupboard. Several well painted water-colours adorned the walls.

"Here's the galley," Greg said, moving ahead. It was separated from the saloon by a hatch. He picked up the percolator and gave it a little shake. "I'm afraid I've finished this. I'll make a fresh lot."

44

"Please don't bother," she said hurriedly. "I can make myself a coffee at the villa."

"I doubt if you'll get back to the villa today." He spoke casually, as though he was in charge of her life.

"What do you mean?" she asked sharply.

"We could spend the day on board."

"The day?" she echoed. "I've no clothes."

"What's wrong with what you have on? You look very nice to me."

"I'll get sunburned – in this."

His mouth twitched. "We could spend all the time out of the sun. There's a very comfortable main cabin.

"Look," said Julie, trying to sound cool and sophisticated, "this is all very amusing but I don't know anything about you."

"You'll know quite a lot about me after you've spent the day with me on board this yacht," he told her, eyes twinkling. "And as to your reputation, if that's what's worrying you, no one would then be able to say you had been aboard a strange yacht with a strange man. Come on, trust me."

"Frankly," she replied, "I don't." She wished he wasn't so incredibly attractive. "Look, I'm going." She flung the towel to the deck and went to the side.

He laughed softly. "You're not, actually." He took her arm and turned her towards the companionway. "Now, to breakfast. How do you like your coffee. Strong? Weak? Black? White? It's brewing now."

She could smell it drifting up from below. "All right," she said, "you win." She allowed him to lead her down into the heart of the vessel.

"Shall we start with a Grand Tour? You've seen the wheelhouse. "Cabins one and two here, opposite each other," Greg said. There were neatly made-up bunks one above the other, a tiny hand basin, and cupboards. "Here's the master cabin. This, as I suggested, is where we could spend the day in order to avoid sunburn."

She spun round, then suddenly they were laughing together once again. Julie looked in astonishment at a big double bed with the headboard of Chinese figures

45

carved in wood and painted gold. There were wall-length wardrobes, a built-in dressing-table. Her feet sank into deep, fluffy pile carpet.

She looked at him narrowly, trying to access him. This could not be his boat. He was a man for a racing yacht, sharp-nosed, high-sailed, narrow and low in the water, with a minimum of space below.

He seemed to read her thoughts for he said, "I didn't design it," as though he was in the habit of designing his yachts.

"I thought you stole it from Fiumicino."

"That's right."

She glanced at him sharply. He wasn't proud of this yacht. His nonsense seemed to be a ruse for distancing himself from it.

"There's a bathroom through there," he said. "That's about it, except for the small cabin in the bow – crew's quarters, though. I don't use a crew except on very long trips. So long as I have someone to help me cast off and tie up, I can manage without. What kind of sailor are you?"

"I don't get seasick, if that's what you mean. And I dare say I'm intelligent enough to do what I'm told." She was suddenly excited, albeit in a nervous kind of way, at the idea of spending the day aboard this luxurious yacht.

"You only live once," he said again as though he read her thoughts. "Where shall we take off for? Gibraltar?" She laughed. "Ischia, then?"

"Mm – that sounds lovely. I've never been there."

He went ahead of her to the galley and set about pouring the coffee.

"Sorry, no bread, but you'll understand I haven't done any marketing this morning. Will a few ship's biscuits and a lump of bully beef do?" He opened a tin marked Fortnum and Mason and shook some delicious-looking little buttery rounds on to a plate, brought a pot of Gentleman's Relish out of a cupboard and a plate of butter from a small refrigerator tucked beneath the bench. "Help yourself to the ship's rations while I get ready to cast off."

"Some ship's biscuits! Some bully beef!"

46

"I'll get her going," he said. Agile as a cat, he swung himself up the companionway.

She tucked happily into the extravagant little snack. Greg had started the engine. She could feel its throb through the deckboards. "What can I do?" she called and went up on deck with the coffee in one hand and biscuit in the other.

He was standing at the wheel, wearing a white yachting cap. He turned his head. "Either steer it away from the jetty as I cast off, or go ashore and cast off yourself while I steer.

"Since I know nothing about boats, I think I might be safer on the jetty. I'd hate to have her bolt with me, leaving you on shore."

"Worry not," he replied laconically. "You'd run out of gas in time. Drag on that stern rope until she's alongside, then jump."

She did as he asked, brought the yacht close in on a small swell and, leaping ashore, unwound the rope from the bollard, tossed it on to the deck, then as the craft swung round, ran to the bow rope and repeated the operation. But she was not quick enough to jump back on board. "Hang on," called Greg.

"Don't worry. I'll swim." Julie dived into the water and swam with long, firm strokes towards the ship's ladder. There was a yell of alarm. Greg cut the engines. He strode furiously out on deck. "Do you want to get sliced up by the propeller?"

Feeling very stupid, Julie climbed aboard. He was no longer the lighthearted philanderer. His handsome face was dark, his mouth hard. "And I thought you looked intelligent," he said scathingly.

Crushed, she could only apologise. "OK," he replied shortly. "Don't do it again." She went to the bow and stood facing out to sea, feeling small. Away in the distance Capri was shrouded in mist. He had started the engines once again. The yacht headed out to sea.

A little while later she felt his hand on her arm. "I'm sorry," he said. "You gave me a fright."

"I deserved it."

"I was too harsh."

"You don't suffer fools gladly. I've been warned. If it's not an idiotic question now, who's driving the boat?"

"I've set the Morse Control. It's an automatic pilot. She'll be OK for a while."

They scudded far out to sea and presently Greg returned to the deckhouse. The mist over Capri was lifting. In the distance, Julie could see the ferry leaving Positano. There were little fishing-boats coming in with their morning catch, engines thudding. She went to join Greg in the deckhouse. "I'm going to get awfully burned."

"Wouldn't you guess I look after my captives? There's suntan lotion in the bathroom. Help yourself."

"Thanks." She went below. There was an expensively perfumed lotion in the cupboard on the wall. She eyed the distinctly feminine product with a wry smile, spread it over her bare skin, put the bottle back and was about to climb up on deck when Greg called, "If you want a scarf for your hair, or a hat, you might find one in the port-side cabin."

Port? Which side was that? She took the one on the right. The wardrobe door slid back to reveal half-a-dozen expensive-looking sun-dresses, a collection of delicate gold and silver sandals. She shut it hurriedly and was slipping quietly across the passage when she heard Greg's footsteps on the companionway. She turned. He was looking at her stonily.

"Don't you know port from starboard?"

Julie's cheeks flamed. "I'm sorry. I didn't mean to pry," she said. He went into the other cabin and took a man's cotton scarf from a drawer. "Here, tie this round your head," he said briskly. They went back on deck and the moment passed.

They cruised past the high, rocky island of Capri with only the gulls for company, swooping and screeching. The coastline was magical with its white villas and orange roofs, its beaches and rocky bluffs. Julie smoothed the suntan oil over her limbs and stretched out on the deck. Greg went

48

back to the wheelhouse, then returned and stretched out beside her. "I hope you tan easily," he said, "because if you don't, you're going to get very burnt."

"I do," she murmured sleepily and the next moment, it seemed, she was wakened by a kick of the engines and the feel of the yacht swinging round. She sat up, startled. There was a sheet spread over her, head to toe. It fell away as she swung erect. Greg was in the wheelhouse. He looked up, smiling.

"Obviously you needed that sleep," he called.

"Obviously I did," she retorted wryly, remembering why she had been awake half the night. "But what a waste!" She looked out on a busy waterfront decked with striped awnings and a long row of restaurants.

"This is the best place I know for fish food," called Greg. I'm going to anchor and we'll have a swim first. OK."

"Thank you for covering me up," she said.

"It's all part of the service," he replied goodnaturedly. "Ready to go?"

The dived overboard to swim far out of the way of the noisy shore crowds. A fishing-boat idled by, dragging its net. The sky was cornflower blue, the sea silkily warm. She said as they floated, their faces turned to the burning sun, eyes closed, "Why, when you had the yacht to sleep aboard, did you go through all that hocus-pocus last night?"

He replied disarmingly, "I wanted to know you. To see what sort of girl would lead Martin Wingate almost to the altar, then ditch him. And perhaps to find out why. Since you ask—" he turned over on his front "—was it vengeance?"

"Why should I feel vengeful against Martin?" she asked.

"Because of his bringing that girl, Antonia, to Paris. That's what it was about, wasn't it? You found out."

In spite of the warmth of the water, Julie felt a cold chill run down her spine. She dived, swam underwater away from him, then surfaced to find him treading water only a yard away.

"You're not going to tell me you were unaware of the fact that he moved Antonia into a flat in Paris just about five minutes after he took up with you?"

So it was true! She felt numbed by the pain of it. She wanted to swim away and lick her wounds all by herself. She wished she hadn't come. She felt angry and upset that he should have brought her here then proceeded to spoil her day.

"Why are you telling me this?" she asked.

"Because there's an old truism which says you have to be cruel to be kind and I suspect you've got your head in the sand about Martin."

"It's none of your business where my head is." She swung round and swam fast to the side of the cruiser, then hauled herself up on deck. He followed her.

As they towelled themselves dry, he said, just as though nothing at all had happened between them, "We can either go ashore to one of the restaurants, or have something here. What would you like?"

She did not want the intimacy of the boat, the two of them alone, Greg asking questions that were too painful to answer. She said, her voice still sharp with hurt, "I would like to go ashore, but I'm not properly dressed." She added, avoiding his eyes, "There seem to be plenty of women's clothes down there. Perhaps I could borrow something."

Without a word he went below and returned with a slip of a dress.

"This would fit anyone," he remarked, tossing it to her.

She picked up the garment and held it against her. It was exactly the right length and, as he had said, would fit anyone. That is, any slim girl with long legs, and the colours would suit anyone with long blonde hair she told herself sardonically, remembering the conversation that escaped from the powder-room at the restaurant last night. She tried to laugh about it as she slipped the garment over her head. The yellow was exactly right for her skin. "And a comb?" she suggested.

"Assuming you now know port from starboard," he replied, unsmiling, "you will find one in my cabin."

"Thank you." Why doesn't he use the master cabin? she asked herself as she went down the companionway and

50

opened the door of the small one from which he had brought the scarf. Again she had the feeling that this yacht did not belong to him. Was she actually aboard a stolen vessel? No, that didn't seem quite right. She was certain now he wasn't a thief. So what was he? A businessman in the City of London, he had said. So why is he interested in looking after me? Did Moira ask him to call on me? If so, why is he not straightforward about it?

There was a comb on a shelf in front of a mirror. She ran it through her hair then hurried back on deck. Greg had fired the engines and they were coming in to one of the jetties to tie up. She thought, he is kind. He covered me up so I wouldn't get sunburnt. He is polite. He is good looking. And I am falling in love. Maybe he went to school with Martin. Maybe he didn't. Maybe he owns this yacht. Maybe he doesn't. I am on holiday. When people are on holiday they fall in love. It is expected. It is allowed. I could stop being a suspicious nineteenth century spinster and have fun. That is what I would like to do. Forget about Martin and the trouble between my parents and me, and have fun.

The yacht nosed gently up against the jetty. She leaped ashore. Greg threw the mooring rope and she wound it round the bollard.

They ate seafood and drank the local wine then went off to sea again. They sunbathed on deck and swam. In the evening they cruised slowly back to the mainland. The sun was going down in a blaze of scarlet and gold behind the crouching lion rock of Capri and a blue dusk lay over the silent water.

Greg said, "You'll dine with me again tonight? I know a very special place." They were standing side-by-side at the wheel. Julie felt sun-soaked to the bone now, as though the day had spread a silken bandage over her wounds. She lifted her face to say yes and he bent down to kiss her lightly on the lips. It was not a lover's kiss. Nor was it demanding. His mouth barely brushed hers. "I'm sure some of the best shipwrecks occur when the captain is kissing one of the crew," he said.

"I'll keep my distance, then." She moved out of reach,

51

but she was smiling. "Yes, let's eat together. And thank you, Greg, for a lovely, lovely day."

She went ashore and climbed up the steep zig-zag path, feeling exhilarated; a little light-headed, perhaps. It was as though she had moved for the moment beyond her troubles.

Greg had told her where to look for a switch that would light up the precipitous path in the rock cliff. She made her way up to the villa, felt in the cleft and found the door key, slipped it into the keyhole and went inside. As she passed through the hall something lying on the stairs caught her eye. An envelope. A telegram from Moira? She hurried to pick it up.

It was indeed a telegram. She slit the envelope and read: *If Strathallan turns up lock the door stop love Moira.*

Julie stood where she was while the warmth of the day drained from her. Lock the door! What did that mean? That Moira didn't want him in her villa? That she, Julie, mustn't have anything to do with him? Why on earth had Moira not been more explicit? Because, knowing how very attractive Greg was, how vulnerable Julie was after her distressing experiences, she didn't trust her with a choice?

Lock the door! This was Moira's villa. She must first of all take the message to mean Greg must not be allowed in, and as the villa was her responsibility she must obey. Now she could look at the message's ambiguity. Don't let him in. Don't have anything to do with him? She thought again of the two women she had overheard talking in the restaurant last night.

Crumpling the telegram in her hand, she went to her room and stood at the window looking out into the darkness of the Bay of Salerno. At the tiny lights on the boats floating at anchor. Far away pin points of gold indicated the rocky island of Capri.

'But isn't this what you wanted to know?' she asked herself unhappily. What about all those women's clothes in the cabin? And the perfumed suntan lotion? Do they belong to his wife? Or some other woman? Wasn't this what she had wanted to find out when she had tried to ring Moira last night? So why the distinct sense of loss? Fool! She brushed a hand across her eyes, wiping away tears that made no sense unless they were self-pity because Greg had lifted her up so high before dashing her down again.

She peeled off her bikini, showered and quickly washed the salt out of her hair. Then she pulled on a pair of trousers and a thin blouse, picked up her shoulder-bag, and with a nervous glance at her watch, tore a page out of her diary. She hesitated only a moment, then wrote: '*I don't want you to feel you have to entertain me. I'm sure you would rather spend the evening with one of your friends. Thanks for the lovely day.*' And she signed it with the initial 'J.' She put the note down on the step with a pebble to hold it, locked the garden door, then let herself out of the villa. A moment later she was in her car, speeding into Positano.

The little town was a hillside of twinkling lights. Julie turned down one of the steep narrow streets and driving slowly, twisting and turning, came to sea level. She parked the car close to the beach and locked it.

The moon by this time had risen. There was enough light to see where she was going. Pushing her hands down into her pockets, she strode off along the beach.

It was cool here with a light breeze off the sea. She walked to the far end of the beach where the cliffs rose, then back again. She walked until she was tired, until her shoes were heavy with sand.

The moon cam up and with it a terrible sense of aloneness. The dark beach stretched out emptily in front of her. She felt empty herself. She kept on walking until she was too tired to go on. I must eat, she said to herself. Perhaps, after that, having examined the alternatives, she would be able to make a decision on what to do. She set off round the narrow, twisting little lanes.

She found a small restaurant where the tables spilled out on to the pavement. A lively, smiling waiter, balancing an enormous tray on one hand, paused to speak to her as she stood in the road considering. "You wish a table, signora?"

She nodded. "Yes, please. For one."

The table he offered her was against a vine-covered wall. As she walked towards it, her eyes roved over the diners, looking with suddenly electric nervousness for a black head, a pair of laughing green eyes.

Greg was not there, but the two women who had been in the restaurant the night before were. They gave her a surreptitious glance, then looked away. As she sat down at the table she had been given nearby one of them spoke to the other in French. "Isn't that the girl who was with Greg last night?"

Well, wasn't this her opportunity? She felt idiotically angry that they should assume, just because of her obvious Englishness, that she did not speak French. She mustered up courage and, turning round, asked, "Do you by any chance know where Greg Strathallan garages his car?"

Momentarily, they looked startled, then pulled themselves together and one of them asked uncertainly, "The Maserati?"

Julie nodded, the slow red of embarrassment rose in her cheeks. She was not good at this sort of thing. Not good at tricking people.

"He has a lock-up place behind Luigi's at Amalfi." They waited for her to go on, their eyes curious.

Julie said, "Thank you," and turned back to her own table. What did it matter? And what did such a reply prove, anyway, she asked herself crossly, except what she already knew. That Greg was a liar. Like Martin.

The women rose, smiling down at her as they left. Julie smiled stiffly back. The waiter came and she ordered spaghetti because she could not be bothered to look at the menu. It was important to eat. That was all. To fill her stomach and give herself strength. She ate quickly, scarcely tasting the food, paid her bill and went back to the car. It was nearly eleven.

She drove up out of the town, parked at the top of the hill where she could look back at the lights and switched off the engine. She sat there waiting for time to pass. Waiting for Greg to give up waiting for her.

At midnight she started up again and drove back to the

54

villa. It was in darkness. She let herself in, switched on the lights from the top of the little stairway and looked down into the hall. She felt the villa was empty. All the same she called, "Greg, are you there?"

When there was no reply, and how could there be, she asked herself, for he did not have a key, she came down into the hall, went to the garden door and opened it. The note had gone.

She went to her room and started tiredly to undress. Tomorrow, she said to herself, I will decide what to do.

Chapter Four

A decision came to her in the half-awake, half-asleep hours. She could not stay in the Villa Rosa with the emotional dilemma that came with it, and the responsibilities it entailed. She was not yet ready to face her parents. One worrying remark of Greg's kept returning to her mind. 'I can't imagine what your father's up to.' It had passed her by in the stress of the moment. Now she wanted to know what he had meant. But in order to find out she would be taking a chance on having to let him into the villa. More than this, how could she explain to him that Moira, whom he said was a friend, had told her to lock the door against him?

Whatever that meant.

She now accepted that her marriage to Martin must have been the deciding factor in the amalgamation of the hotels. But why? What did Greg know that she didn't? Or had he merely been listening to City speculation? I will not marry a man I don't respect in order to further my parents' business interests, she said to herself. And then she remembered how much she owed to the hotels. But I also have put in a great deal, she thought. I have worked long hours. Done my share. I do not believe I should be sacrificed . . . Her mind continued to go round and round until at last she drifted off to sleep.

In the morning she knew what she would do. It was six o'clock when she wakened. She slid out of bed, packed her case, made herself a cup of coffee and left. She drove inland where yachts do not go. She followed road signs to strange places. Sannita. Ariano Irpino. Melfi. She stopped at little villages. Ate pizzas at tiny pavement cafés, smiling at the friendly locals, making signs that she didn't speak their language. And they, of course, did not speak hers. She left her car at roadsides and walked beside rivers. Basked in the sun. Kept her mind blank. She stayed the night in village houses with signs outside saying they had rooms to let. *Camera Libera.* It was like leaving one's life behind.

By the end of the week she knew what to do next. She would return to London and try to find herself a job in the only world she knew, hotel management. She drove to Naples airport, relinquished the car and took a plane to Heathrow.

Dan Barlow was an old friend. They had known each other since they were children. He also knew Martin, perhaps better than Julie did for they were at university together. His family owned the Gideon Hotel in Kensington. She went straight there with her suitcase in her hand and asked to speak to Dan. He received her with surprise.

"Sit down, Julie. Here, let me take your bag." He put it by the door then resumed his seat behind the desk. "So!" he said, smiling uncertainly.

She came straight to the point. "I'm looking for a job, Dan."

His fingers tap-tapped on the desk top, his generous mouth turned down. His grey eyes held a faint look of alarm. "Don't you want to tell me anything? I only know what was in the gossip columns."

She said, "Oh hell! I hadn't thought of that."

"It's nothing personal," Dan said consolingly. "It's the proposed merger that creates interest. Is it or isn't it going ahead? That's what they're asking."

"It's nothing to do with me."

"The papers seem to think it has a hell of a lot to do with you. You must know it was in the financial pages that Martin's father and yours had settled their differences and were proposing amalgamation. You've got to be aware that your bust-up with Martin would provoke speculation in case it should affect that."

She sat silent. Of course this was how it was going to be. Everyone in the hotel business would want the inside story. What story? The one she was hiding from. The

57

one she didn't want to know the answer to. Why the amalgamation should be affected by their marriage. But she couldn't explain why she had run away. Not without telling everyone that Martin was a liar and a cheat. That he was cheating on his father as well as on his fiancée.

"I just felt that Martin and I didn't know each other well enough," she temporised.

"Perhaps you didn't," Dan acceded. And then he added with surprising feeling, "It was foolish to come between Antonia and Martin."

"Everyone has past girlfriends. He told me the affair was over. I didn't come between them."

Dan pushed himself upright in his chair, his eyes incredulous. "But everyone in town knew he was seeing her!"

"Everyone but me," she retorted bitterly, reliving the pain of it. "Remember I was working in Le Septre in Paris. Martin was travelling back and forth to London but spending more time in Paris. That, I imagine, is why he brought Antonia over. He evidently thought he could have both of us." She told him how Antonia had written to her mother but that she had been kept in the dark. "She showed the letter to me the night I broke off the engagement."

"And that's why?"

"No. It's more complex than that," Julie replied evasively, evading the issue of Martin's going into antiques. "But he was cheating on me, Dan. I know you're a friend of both of them, but you're also a friend of mine. Couldn't you have told me he hadn't finished with Antonia?" She felt lonely and alone. It seemed to her that all her friends had let her down.

Dan looked uncomfortable. "People don't like to interfere," he said.

"Even when he's cheating on two women? In marrying me he was cheating on Antonia. She's a friend of yours too, it seems. Wouldn't you like to help her?"

"She must have been willing to go along with it," he said. "After all, she did know. Everyone knew he was going to marry you. What happened between Martin and Antonia is their business. No, of course I wouldn't interfere, you must know that." He picked up a pen and began to doodle on his pad. "We all expected he would marry Antonia. After all, they've been together for years."

For years! How little she had known of this man when she promised to marry him!

What kind of woman was this, Julie wondered bleakly, who would stand aside while the man she loved married someone else? Watching Dan with his head down concentrating on the ink scribblings on his pad she relented. It was true, this was nobody's business but the people concerned. She understood that he could not interfere.

"I've come to ask you for a job."

"It's not up to me. You'll have to talk to my father. I'll tell you what. There is a possibility of a temporary job, now I come to think about it. Our Miss Turnbull has been wanting to get away for some time to look after her mother who's terminally ill. I could let her go if I had somebody experienced to take over. But as I said, it's not up to me."

"I'll talk to your father," said Julie eagerly.

Mr Barlow was an older edition of Dan. Grey eyes, a chunky frame. "I'd be very happy to take you on temporarily, Julie," he said and she noted the very faint emphasis on the word temporarily. Of course he had no wish to run foul of her father. She thanked him warmly.

"You're easier to talk to than Dan," she said, adding bitterly, "He doesn't seem to be my friend any more."

"You must understand that Dan and his friends knew Antonia when they were undergraduates. She was secretary to one of the professors, you know."

"No. I didn't know."

"They all went out together, before you came on the scene."

"So I'm the interloper." She couldn't keep the misery out of her voice.

"Not that," Mr Barlow replied. "It's all about business, isn't it?" He added hurriedly, "I'm not saying Martin doesn't love you. I'm taking the City view."

It was not going to be easy to live with the fact that everyone knew Martin had only wanted to marry her for business reasons. That all his friends were sorry for Antonia.

She gave Dan's father a bleak look. "So you're going to give me the job?"

He smiled. He was kind. "Yes, my dear. Bearing in mind that it's temporary, of course."

That evening, late, she went round to the Hotel Merrion. After eleven, if she was quick getting across the ground floor, she was unlikely to run into anyone but the desk clerk, and guests. Luckily, the desk was actually unmanned as she came into the foyer so she slipped into the lift and went up to the family's private apartments. She hung up her holiday gear and collected working clothes. She also rang Moira. Moira kept late hours. There was no reply so she left a message on the answering machine giving the Gideon's number.

When she came down the clerk was there but he was on the telephone. His back was turned. She slipped out of the revolving doors with her bag and called a taxi.

She started work at the Gideon right away. It was not an exciting job, but it paid well and it was work for which she had been trained. Dan's father gave her a room, and a tiny sitting-room that was also her office, on the first floor. She divided her time between this refuge and the busy reception desk on the ground floor. She worked long hours, deliberately tiring herself out so that she would not lie awake at night.

The Gideon's guests were mainly from abroad. But they also did conferences. When the conference room was in use Julie's work doubled. She enjoyed the bustle, the sorting out of innumerable difficulties that arose in the pressurised rush of a three-day, three-night gathering.

So many things could go wrong so easily, the achievement of perfection or even near perfection was a challenge that took her out of her personal world and gave her no time to think. Lost programmes, transport failing to turn up for speakers needing to catch a train or plane, catering arrangements coming unstuck – they were all grist to the mill of the moment.

60

Her own troubles had to be faced and would be faced, when she had enough confidence back. Not yet. Once or twice she found herself recalling that blissful day of sun and sea on the yacht with Greg Strathallan, but she quickly thrust the memory out of her mind. Escapism, that's what that day had been, she told herself wryly. Anyone would have looked attractive to her in her very vulnerable state.

She had been at the hotel for only a short time when the auditors came to do the books. "Oh, no!" she exclaimed, not trying to hide her dismay when Dan told her the name of the firm, and when they would be arriving.

"Why? What's wrong, Julie? They're a good firm," he protested.

"They're Father's auditors! Old Leonard Crombie will certainly tell my parents I'm here. Can I have a few days off? Or stay out of sight?"

"They will have to know," Dan reminded her sensibly. "They'll see your name on papers. And besides," he added, "isn't it about time you got in touch with your parents to tell them you're OK? I know you've had a bad time, but haven't they, too? You left them with a cancelled wedding on their hands."

"I cancelled the wedding," Julie retorted. "I didn't leave them with anything. Only their—" She stopped abruptly with a hand to her mouth. Only their consciences, she had been going to say. But she mustn't. That was private, between them and her when she had plucked up the courage to face them again.

"What did you leave them with?" Dan looked at her sideways.

"I'll leave you to think that out for yourself. And you can," she said, "if you like to put your mind to it."

He gave her an enigmatic look but did not reply.

Thinking of Greg reminded her that Moira had not rung back. Moira often didn't ring back for days, and sometimes, when she was very busy, not at all. At least she knew Julie had left the villa. Anyway, she did not want that telegram explained. She wanted to keep the memory of the episode in Positano in her memory. To bask in what might have been if she had not panicked.

The auditors came. Julie carried the books into the office behind Reception where Mr Crombie was to work.

Leonard Crombie's eyebrows went up in a startled arch. "Julie! What are you doing here?"

"Helping out." She put down her burden with a bump and turned away, but he caught her by the arm. He was a large man, grey-haired, with piercing blue eyes. He had children the same age as herself who had also been on the guest list. "Everyone wants to know where you are, Julie. Your parents are anxious."

She moved away and he released his grip. "Give them a call, love," he said persuasively. "They're all in London."

"All?" she asked warily.

"Martin, too." He looked at her kindly, and with concern.

"I'm not ready to talk to my parents," she said distinctly. "I'm sorry, but I need time. I must ask you not to tell them I'm here." She did not want to tell him about the sense of betrayal she lived with. That she was not ready to talk to her father about. Nor prepared to forgive. To be betrayed by your lover is bad enough, to be betrayed by your parents is the final straw, she could have said.

He looked at her sadly.

"How can I not, dear?"

"You can," she said. She tried to smile at him but the tension in her caused the smile to twist and falter. "You can choose to be loyal to me instead of being loyal to them. You've known me since I was a little girl, Mr Crombie, but I'm not a little girl now."

Later that day, while still feeling disturbed from the encounter, she realised she should have telephoned Moira. She picked up the receiver and dialled.

"*Cherie!*" Moira exclaimed. "Where are you?"

As if she didn't know!

Julie told her, resisting the temptation to say she had left a message on the answer machine.

"So you met my friend Greg!"

"Your friend!" Julie exclaimed.

"A very old friend. I hope you took my advice and gave him the push, as you would say."

"I did. But now I wonder what you meant."

"I meant you must not get involved with that one."

"You didn't mean I should not allow him in the villa?" Julie's voice rose in surprise.

"Of course I meant it."

"Why, since he is a friend of yours? I thought he must be a criminal or something."

"Perhaps he is. You are in enough trouble without getting involved with him. He is in enough trouble without getting involved with you," said Moira. "Give me your telephone number, *cherie* and I will ring you another time. At the moment I have someone I must attend to."

Julie sat down and stared into space. After a while she shook her head, picked up the list of names for next week's conference and began sorting out the rooms. When it was one-thirty in the morning and she was too tired to think any more she tidied up her desk and went to bed. As she was drifting off to sleep, in that lucid moment just before oblivion, she remembered she had forgotten to ask Mr Crombie not to tell Martin where she was living.

A day or two later when a call came from downstairs saying there was someone to see her who would not give his name she asked, "Is he thinnish, about twenty-eight, with blond hair?" and was taken aback to find her voice trembling.

"Yes."

"I'm sorry," she said, "but I cannot see him. Please tell him I'm not available." She put the receiver down. But Martin came again and again and at last someone downstairs, bored, embarrassed or interfering, told him where he could find her. He opened the door without knocking and marched in. She thought she had developed an impregnable outer crust but when she looked at him she felt a stab of real pain.

"Martin!" She jumped up, caught her skirt on the arm

of the chair, ripped some stitches as she jerked it free, and spoke angrily, "You've no right to burst in on me like this."

He smiled at her in that endearing way he had. "I had to see you," he said. "I have to talk to you."

Was that actually misery in his tawny eyes? She fought an upsurge of sympathy. "What do you want to talk about? Antonia?" She stood rigidly behind her desk, chin high.

"Don't be like that, Julie. It was you I wanted to marry. I still want to marry you."

She put a hand over her heart as though she could ease its thumping. "On your terms, yes. Only the terms aren't good enough. When I marry I don't want to be part of a harem." There, she had said it!

His face clouded, he began to look outraged, then laughed a little, awkwardly. "What on earth are you talking about?"

"About the fact that Antonia wrote to my mother, warning her that you would never let her go." She felt again the stunning blow of remembered shock. "I don't know Antonia but I don't believe any girl would say such a thing if it wasn't true. I mean, Martin—" she bit her lip and looked up at him through suddenly tear-filled eyes, "When a girl is cast aside, believe me, she knows it. You didn't cast Antonia aside."

They stared at each other. The silence hit Julie like a blow. She said, and her voice emerged shakily, "Now, if you don't mind, I've work to do. Will you please go?"

He didn't move. "I've known Antonia for a long time. A man doesn't drop all his old friends when he marries." Martin said what he had said before, in a carefully reasonable voice. "You're being very possessive, Julie."

"He doesn't move his long-term lover into an apart-ment nearby so that he can go back to her anytime he has a tiff with his wife," she flared, and recognised with chagrin that the hurt was showing in the trembling of her voice. "If it's being possessive to object, then I am that." If only he would say Antonia had moved to Paris without his knowledge, she thought, perhaps they could talk.

But he didn't. He merely looked at her with those melting eyes and said, "Let's start again, shall we?"

"Please go away. I never want to see you again."

At the door he turned. "I love you, Julie, and I want you still. I'll be in touch," he said.

When he had gone, she went to the window and stood staring down into the street below, looking at the evenng traffic through a blur of tears. 'It's only your pride that's hurt.' She waited to be convinced and there was nothing. Only pain. The enigma of Martin, the warmth of him, the lively, happy, complex, clever Martin who had flattered his way so expertly into her heart.

There was a gentle tap at the door. Oh no! If she did not answer he might go away. But the door opened and Dan came in carrying two brandy glasses. He put them down on the desk. "Here, try this," he said. He handed her one and took the other himself. "Cheers." Then with a wry grimace: "If that's the right word."

She sipped the burning liquid in silence. It caught at her throat and made her cough.

After a while Dan said, "I know it's embarrassing for you. Facing people, I mean. But you haven't been out once since you've been here. You can't go on like this."

She flicked her hair back from her face and looked at Dan. "He seemed genuinely to want me back."

"Are you going to him?"

"I can't."

"Yet you say he wants you, and you obviously love him, otherwise you wouldn't be so upset."

She replied in a rush, "You know Antonia, Dan. You've known her a long time. What do you advise me to do?" She watched his still face, suddenly wondering if he had poured a brandy for Antonia the day Martin announced his engagement to her.

"Life's tough," he said with a philosophical shrug. "How we deal with it is up to us. I don't want you to work tonight. I don't think you should, I'll get you another brandy. And then I'll take you out to dinner."

"You're a very good friend," she said, smiling at him.

He smiled back. "That's what makes life good, isn't it? Having friends. Go and change now if that's what you want to do and I'll meet you in the foyer in – how long?"

"Half an hour."

"Right."

She tidied away her papers and went to her room to change. She put on a black dress she had brought from the Merrion and as she did so she wondered if her mother had been to her room and noticed that some of her clothes were gone. Probably not. She looked at herself in the full length mirror as she brushed her hair. The black dress accentuated her slimness. She had lost weight. And its brief skirt showed up the length of her legs. Long fair hair and long legs, she thought and wondered why at that moment she should remember those two women with the gleaming gold necklaces who had been gossiping about Greg in the powder-room at Positano. Well, this was a very different scene. She picked up her bag and went downstairs. Dan was waiting in the foyer.

At the moment they met his father came hurrying out of his office. "You're not going out?" he asked in dismay.

"Yes. I'm taking Julie to dinner."

Mr Barlow said, "Something's come up. There's been a banquet booking made for Tuesday and they're threatening to cancel. I can't deal with it myself."

"Can't it wait till morning?"

"No. But I don't want to spoil things for you. Would you mind having your meal here? Then you'd be on call to help sort it out when they ring back. I'd be very grateful if you would."

Dan looked at Julie apologetically. "Do you mind?"

"Of course not." She was transparently grateful, for she had been dreading going out to a restaurant where she might meet friends, or glimpse acquaintances who might be whispering about her.

The dining-room was full. Without looking to right or left Julie went straight to the reserved family table in the

66

corner and sat down with her back to the room. Dan laughed softly, sympathetically. "You can't live like a hermit, Julie."

She gave him a rueful smile. "I can try."

The waiter came with the menu. "You'd better have something filling," Dan said. "Do you know you've lost weight?"

"I was noticing that. Remembering I was a bit fatter before I ran away to Positano. All right, I'll have thick soup and lamb cutlets with lots of potato."

"So that's where you went," Dan commented as he handed the menu back. "You didn't say."

"Didn't I?"

He grinned. "You know very well you didn't. You've become very secretive, Julie."

"I'm sorry." She knew why she had kept the Positano experience to herself, all the reasons, secret as well as embarrassing. That little bit of warmth that had crept into her heart the day she and Greg cruised to Ischia was something she wanted to hold against the bleak loneliness of her present existence.

"What did you do there?" Dan asked.

"I had a couple of wonderful seafood meals, some swims, and a lot of driving." She looked down at the white table cloth, musing. "And somebody said I had long legs and long fair hair."

Dan laughed. "So you have. Tell me about that? It's not quite a compliment. More a fact. But I dare say it pleased you."

"It didn't, actually," She looked down, fingering her fork.

"Go on. I'm intrigued."

"It was a disturbing experience. I'll tell you one day." She corrected herself, "Maybe I'll tell you one day."

"You're full of secrets, aren't you?"

"No," she said. "I'm hurt. I'm scared of my own shadow. Let me hide, Dan."

"OK. Sorry. I didn't mean to pry." He lifted his head and allowed his glance to rove round the room. Julie looked at the wall, carefully avoiding the mirror just above eye-level on the wall.

Dan said good-humouredly, "Shall I tell you who's here?"

"So long as it doesn't scare me." She looked wry.

"OK. I'll tell you about a chap who has me a bit baffled. I don't know him but I know him by sight and by reputation. He's been here for dinner for the last four evenings, and once for lunch," Dan said. "I'm puzzled because I've never seen him here before."

"Why don't you speak to him?"

"I shall. I've been busy when I glimpsed him, and each time it was when he was leaving. But I will."

"You'll probably find out he has just discovered your good food," said Julie, smiling. "What's interesting about him?" She was accustomed to hotel gossip. Enjoyed it.

"He made a lot of money in marine insurance. Then he got besotted with some girl and desperately wanted to marry her. She made all sorts of conditions, then shortly after she got the wedding ring on her finger, she drowned herself. Or was murdered."

"No!"

"Yes." He grinned. "That brought you to life. Don't look round. He'll see you."

"Tell me more."

"He was questioned by the police and that got into the papers. But later it was said she had gone off to South America with a lover. I can't imagine why he has started eating here, unless he wants a quiet place to hide where he won't meet his friends, or where the media won't find him."

Julie said drily, "I expect that's it. For the same reason I asked you for a job. The Gideon doesn't attract gossip columnists." She looked at him, her eyes soft. "You're very kind, aren't you, Dan?"

Briskly, he brushed the compliment aside. "Let's say I'm grateful my own life's going well."

They were half-way through the first course when Dan was called away to deal with the double booking. As the waitress took his plate to keep it hot, Julie, forgetting about

68

the mirror, glanced idly up and met a small sea of faces. Then she froze, for a man was walking across the dining-room towards her. He came right up to her table, pulled out Dan's chair and sat down. "Well, Julie?"

She stared at him. She was speechless. He looked quite different in a business suit with a carefully knotted and tasteful silk tie, his hair smooth, the intense suntan already beginning to fade. That wonderful day, the excitement, the warmth and the healing balm of it came sweeping back and with it a picture of Greg like a dark Greek god at the helm of the yacht, stripped to the waist with the wind in his hair.

"How did you know I was here?"

"You can find out anything if you really want to. I went to see Moira in Paris. She wouldn't give me your number." A mischievous look came into his eyes. "She went to get her things and while her back was turned I took a quick look at her telephone pad. There it was. It wasn't difficult, when I got back to London, to find out where the number belonged. Hotel Gideon, said the desk clerk when I dialled, so I hopped in my car and came over to dinner."

"Why didn't you ask for me?"

"Would you, if you had gone to collect a girl to take her out to eat and found a note telling you to get lost?"

Julie flushed. "That was Moira." And suddenly she knew why. Knew that he was the man Dan had been gossiping about. Certainly he was the man the women had been discussing in the powder-room at Positano when they mentioned the police. No wonder Moira didn't want them to get together, two people in trouble. Now she understood the reason for the terse telegram and the reason Moira had not rung back. There was only a certain distance one could go when interfering in other people's lives. Dan had shown her that. She said breathlessly, "I imagine Moira thinks I've got enough on my plate without getting involved with you."

He let that pass. "So, why are you here?"

"I'm working. It's temporary, while I sort myself out."

69

"You've lost weight. And you've been crying."

She laughed shakily. "Oh Greg, you are the most downright person!" She thought she ought to send him away but instead she blurted out, "Martin found me today. That's why I'm here. Dan Barlow is treating me to dinner to cheer me up."

"Did Martin ask you to come back?"

She nodded.

"And?"

She shook her head.

"Do you love him?"

"Oh Greg!" He was taking her over again, the way he had in Italy. She was frightened but even so she did not want to send him away. "Why doesn't Moira want us to be friends?"

"I thought you must know that." He looked her straight in the eyes.

"I don't."

"Let's ignore her, shall we? I understand you haven't been to see your parents."

"What do you mean? How do you know?"

He said, as though this was a perfectly reasonable thing to do, "I telephoned them."

"You *what*!"

"I said I knew Martin, which is true. I knew him when we were at prep school. I didn't have to say I've not bothered with him since we were twelve." His eyes were innocent, his mouth twitching.

"What did they say?"

"That you had gone off without leaving an address. Your mother sounded sad. I said if I could find you I'd bring you to see them."

"You *what*!" she exclaimed again, breathlessly this time. She felt taken over.

He was suddenly grave. "They're intensely worried about you." He put a hand over hers on the table. "Julie, sometimes things can go badly wrong and you're left wishing you had done the right thing when you had the chance."

She was deeply touched. This was a new side to him. She

wondered if he was thinking of his own troubles. She felt a little of his courage seeping into her. "I will go and see my parents," she said.

"Tomorrow night? I'd like to take you out to dinner." And then, without waiting for her agreement added, "I'll pick you up here at seven-thirty."

"Oh!" she breathed and the magic of that dinner in Positano spiralled around her. She felt her cheeks grow warm, felt the warmth spreading through her. It wouldn't hurt to go, just once, would it? No, she must not. He was married. Besotted with his wife. She floundered for an excuse, knocked her bag to the floor and bumped her head against his while retrieving it.

"Come out of the sand, Miss Ostrich," Greg said softly in her ear.

Out of the sand! It seemed more like out of Martin's frying-pan into Greg's fire!

"We'll have dinner, then I'll deliver you to the Merrion afterwards. You may be a parent yourself one day," Greg said and softened the remark with a smile.

"Did my mother ask you to bring me to see them?" she asked edgily.

"No. One doesn't ask strangers that kind of thing. I told you I offered. So, that's a date," Greg said as though she had agreed. "It's a tough old life. Too tough to get through on your own, sometimes." He pushed back his chair.

There was a hand on Julie's shoulder. She swung round to see Dan had returned. Greg rose.

"Don't go," Dan protested.

"I must." Greg nodded briefly and walked towards the door.

Dan looked bemused as he resumed his chair. "So you know the notorious Strathallan. Or was he trying to pick you up?"

Julie clasped her hands together so tightly the nails bit into her palms. "I met him in Italy. I'd no idea he was the man you were speaking about." She told him Greg was a friend of Moira Ferroni who had loaned her the

71

Villa Rosa. "She was making my wedding dress," Julie said wryly.

"Wheels within wheels, eh?"

She smiled at him with affection. Dan's triteness was a comfort in her turbulent life. "It was Greg you were talking about, wasn't it? He's the man whose wife has disappeared?"

He nodded. "Perhaps I shouldn't have. How was I to know he was a friend of yours? So he's been here looking for you? Oh Julie."

"Don't Oh Julie me," she snapped, then burst out laughing. "I'm sorry. I'm feeling a little lightheaded."

"I'm sorry, too," Dan replied, "that you're feeling lightheaded over a chap who is under suspicion for murdering his wife."

She sobered.

"I take it he's the one who gave you the disturbing experience in Positano." She looked at him ruefully. "The one who talked of long legs and long hair?"

"Actually not. Did you know his wife, Dan?"

Dan shook his head. "I told you. I don't even know him."

"So you wouldn't know if she answered that description? Long legs and long fair hair."

"What I know is gossip. You know how gossip filters through hotels."

She did. "He's very rich. I went aboard his yacht. It really is palatial."

"So I believe. That was one of the conditions of this girl, Samantha, marrying him. That he sell his racing yacht and buy a floating palace for her. She was evidently a very demanding lady."

So that's why he doesn't like it! "Her clothes are still there," whispered Julie. She didn't know why she was saying this. Did she want to be talked out of seeing Greg tomorrow?

"So that's why he has been eating here," Dan said. "I twig. But why didn't he ask for you?"

She told him.

72

"If I were you I'd have left it at that."

The waiter came with the menu before she could reply. She looked down the list, only half taking it in.

"I'd advise chocolate cake," said Dan. "That's fattening."

She folded the menu and smiled wanly at him. "Chocolate cake it is."

Chapter Five

It rained all that day. Soft, warm rain that would be good for the crops and gardens. Nobody minded for there had been scarcely any since spring.

Dressed and waiting for Greg the following evening, Julie caught a glimpse of herself in the mirror in the foyer. She was wearing her most flattering dress. Her long legs emerged from a tiny skirt, her long fair hair was brushed out over her shoulders. She went out on to the pavement.

"You look great," said Dan dashing in from the rain, pausing to furl his umbrella. Her eyes shone. She knew she looked great. He came up close to her and whispered in her ear. "Watch it, though."

She laughed and touched his cheek. "Thanks for the advice."

"Why are you waiting here?"

"Partly because I don't want to hold him up, and partly because we live in a goldfish bowl. It's gone round the staff like wildfire that Martin came in yesterday. I thought I wouldn't add to the excitement by having Greg come to the desk and ask for me."

He chuckled. "Oh come on, give them their share of fun."

At that moment a long, sleek car swept up to the front door. "Whew!" said Dan. "A Maserati! Here, take my brolly."

"Thanks." She snatched it and ran.

Greg stopped half way out of the driving seat, sank back and leaned across to open the passenger door. "Not only ready but early," he said approvingly as she dived in out of the rain.

Julie shot him a quick look, glimpsing in his surprise a picture of his wife – who had long fair hair and long legs? delaying him for hours. Perhaps that was part of the fascination of some women, she found herself thinking wryly as she settled into her comfortable seat. Perhaps Antonia keeps Martin waiting. Perhaps I shouldn't be so available, trying to please.

"How do you like my car?" he asked.

She heard the pride in his voice and was immediately reminded that he had been apologetic about his yacht. "I love it," she said then asked carefully, "Presumably you drove it to Italy."

"I drive it everywhere. Wouldn't you if you had a Maserati?"

She laughed because of his little-boy enthusiasm. "So it's new?"

"Oh no. But you never get used to having this kind of car. I don't believe in taking the good things of life for granted."

She wasn't sure what he was telling her. They crawled along through the traffic in the rain. "Why did you pretend you didn't have a car in Positano?" There, it was out. She felt she had to know.

"You didn't ask."

She said edgily, "You led me to believe you use public transport."

"Led you to believe!" He frowned. "I do use public transport. My garage is in Amalfi because I normally keep *Neptuna* there. If I've left her elsewhere, as happened when you were at the villa, I get to her by bus."

She laughed, because he was full of surprises. She would have thought he was a taxi man. He gave her a quick look and joined in. "Life is often more simple than it seems," he said.

She suddenly realised where they were. "Hey! Where are you taking me?" Greg was steering the car into the curb. Ahead stood the white columned portico of the Hotel Merrion.

He switched off the engine. "I think you had better get the meeting with your parents over first."

75

She panicked. "I thought we'd go afterwards."

"It would mean a rushed dinner. Besides, if it's a difficult meeting, you'll need someone to talk to afterwards."

She liked the way he had taken her over. His strength and right thinking made her feel safe. She almost had her sense of humour back. She tried it out. "I thought I was going to face up to them fortified with food and strong drink."

He grinned. "With a clear head you'll know better what to say. When you think about it, by mixing up the times I've saved you hours of apprehension." He jumped out and came round to open her door. "I'll wait in the bar," he said.

The Merrion was a five-storey hotel, quietly grand without being ostentatious. It had catered for whole generations of families, changing little with the years. She went through the revolving glass doors, spoke to the desk clerk and swiftly crossed to the lift. She let herself in with her own key.

Her mother was sitting on the sofa in the drawing room wearing one of her long gowns. Her *gros point* lay in her lap. She looked up in surprise. "Julie!" she exclaimed delightedly, putting her work down and rising to her feet.

Julie flung her coat down on a velvet armchair and embraced her.

"How lovely to see you! Why didn't you tell us . . ."

"Return of the prodigal daughter." Neil Creighton was standing in the doorway that led to his study, not looking welcoming at all. "And where have you been?" He was dressed in light trousers, and an open necked shirt. Ignoring his sarcasm she went to him and kissed his cool cheek. "I'm very pleased to see you," he said, showing no warmth. "Perhaps I should say relieved. And now, I hope you're going to tell us where you've been. Sit down." He pointed to the sofa.

Deliberately, she went to stand at one of the long windows, then turned to face them. She said in as cool a voice as she could manage, "I'm staying with a friend. And I've seen Martin. I've asked him about Antonia. He still wants to marry me but he won't give her up."

76

She waited for her father's reply. Knew what it should be. 'This is preposterous' was surely what any loving father would say. After a moment's silence he asked instead, "Why should he drop all his old friends?"

She recognised Martin's argument, knew her father had talked to him, and been taken in. "You wouldn't want him tied to your apron strings, would you, Julie?"

She bit back her outrage. "Yes," she retorted, "if being tied to my apron strings is the only way I can keep his mistress out."

"Mistress!" Her father uttered a brisk laugh. "What nonsense."

"Such an old-fashioned word," commented her mother indulgently. "Aren't you romanticising, dear?"

Julie felt chilled. I won't marry Martin unless he's prepared to give up Antonia."

She saw her father's lips tightening.

"In spite of what you've done to him," he said, "he's very much in love with you."

"What *I* have done!"

Julie cast round desperately for an argument he would understand.

"Don't you want to please your father, Julie?" her mother asked gently.

"Not if he wants me to share my husband with another woman. No."

"Julie, my dear, this is wild talk," said her father, adopting a reasonable tone. "Oliver Wingate and I have had discussions and, of course, I've asked him about Antonia. He assures me that Martin never intended to marry her."

"I don't know about that," Julie answered, running a hand through her hair in her distress, "but I believe he never intended to give her up. I believe what she said in the letter to Mother was true – that he would always love her. People say . . ."

"People say what?"

"Everybody – all their friends from Martin's university days knew about Martin and Antonia. I'm the only one who

77

didn't know they were still seeing each other. They have been very close for a long time, I'm told. A long time, Father. You've got to believe me."

"What are you saying? That he intended to marry you, get control of the amalgamated hotels, then divorce you and marry Antonia?" Neil Creighton's pale eyes seemed to grow paler as his colour rose. "If you make accusations like that, Julie, you've got to substantiate them."

"I haven't made that accusation," Julie said looking hard at him. "You did. And it gives me something to think about. Under the present divorce system there would be a division of the spoils. But I understood you thought the Silvine is worth all three of ours so I don't see that applies."

"In their present rather run-down state. Yes, I think that might be true."

Run-down! They were not. This was surely Wingate talk. She tried him out. "Why don't we refurbish, then?"

He hesitated and she waited, watching his face. But he changed the subject. "We're not talking business now, we're talking about you and Martin. I beg you not to be silly about his friendship with this girl."

"All right, I'll stop being silly," she said in an even voice. "But I do have to say if he won't break off with Antonia, then he's not in love with me."

"I think you've got your wires crossed."

"And do you know what I think," Julie retorted, "that you don't trust Martin either. So why do you want him to marry me?"

Her father's face closed.

"All right," she said, "you don't want to talk to me about it. So there's no point in any more discussion. Marriage, as I understand it, is about two people loving each other. You two love each other, so you should understand. I want to have a marriage like yours." She looked directly at her mother. "Would you tolerate Father's having a mistress?"

"Julie, dear," her mother laughed softly, "you're being ridiculous."

"You're dishing out red herrings," snapped her father. He went to the cabinet and poured himself a whisky.

"Why don't you offer us a drink?" Julie asked.

Her mother looked as though she was going to cry. "Julie, dear—"

"Julie dear is old enough to drink."

Her father said severely, "If you will stop being angry I will pour you a sherry."

She laughed but without humour. "I'd prefer a gin, and while you treat me like a small child I don't feel obliged to stop being angry."

He poured the drink in silence.

"What I am saying," Julie went on, "is that if you're in trouble, and I'm old enough and responsible enough to do the work I do for you in three hotels, then I'm old enough to have your confidence."

Her father handed her the gin. "All right," he said. "Oliver Wingate has threatened to break me if this amalgamation doesn't go through."

Julie's head came up. "How can he do that?"

"He can."

Her eyes narrowed. "And you're not going to tell me how?" When he didn't answer she said, "Hadn't he better talk to his son before he starts threatening you?"

"What are you saying?"

"I told you Martin never intended to work seriously for his father and you. Have you forgotten that the original cause of the rift was not Antonia but the fact that he not only wouldn't work in hotels but intended to take me away as well to help with his antiques business?"

"He says that's not true."

"Of course he would deny it," she said bitterly, "and there's no proof." They were back to square one.

Her mother cast an apprehensive look at her husband, then turned back to Julie. "Will you talk to Martin, dear?"

"I'll talk to him," she said. She sipped her drink. She did not say she would talk to him about marriage. But how could one say to a man, 'Your father has threatened to break mine.' How? Why? She imagined Martin laughing. She heard him say, 'Ask your father what he has done to make himself vulnerable.'

79

Her father was suggesting, "We could call him up now."

"No." Julie put her glass down. "I'll call him tomorrow. She turned to them and included them both in her smile, "I'm a big girl now, as I said. I make my own phone calls. That's something I'd like you to think about after I've gone, too. I'm grateful for everything you've done for me, but I believe I've done a good job in return. Think about that." She bent over and kissed her mother. "I've got to go now."

Her father said, "I'll see you out."

"No, please."

But he came with her to the lift and stepped in. "I'll get you a taxi," he said.

"I don't want a taxi. I'll walk."

"It's raining, Julie," he protested.

"It stopped some time ago."

But he stepped out of the lift with her and accompanied her across the foyer. She heaved a huge sigh and sent up a small prayer that Greg would stay out of sight. But as they came through the swing doors he was standing there, so obviously waiting for her that she was obliged to introduce them.

Her father shook Greg's hand then with set face turned and walked back into the hotel. She ran after him, caught him at the lift. He swung round and said in a low, furious voice, "So that's why you didn't want me to come down! Now I see why you don't want to marry Martin! All this codswallop about him having a mistress! There's another man . . ."

Julie opened her mouth to explain. There were so many things she could say. 'He's married. I scarcely know him. He is merely being kind. It was he who made me come and see you.' But her father's anger had taken him out of her reach. And anyway, had not her protests about Antonia lost their validity now?

The lift doors opened and her father stepped in. She stood mutely while they closed after him. When she turned Greg was standing behind her.

"Shall I go up and talk to him?"

"No," she said. "No. It wouldn't do any good." And

possibly, she thought, if her parents also knew the gossip about Greg, it might do a great deal of harm. Gossip was rife in the hotel business and her mother had very little to do but listen to it.

"I'm sorry. I didn't dream you wouldn't come down alone. There was no one in the bar and the barman was very chatty. When he asked if I was waiting for someone I thought I'd better make myself scarce before I started rumours."

"I sometimes think life is one enormous trap," she said grimly. "That we're only here on earth to solve problems."

Greg slipped a hand under her elbow. "Yes, one may as well be philosophical about it. Come on. We're going dancing. I've booked a table at El Rico's because it's so dark there no one will recognise us. And the food's great."

El Rico's was indeed dark and Julie was grateful. Greg was a good dancer. Once, he bent over and kissed her on the forehead. She said swiftly, "I don't want to get involved, Greg. You're not in a position to get involved, and nor am I."

"What did Moira tell you?"

"Nothing."

"Just to take avoidance tactics?"

"That's it."

They walked back to their table. The waiter was there with the soup. Greg tasted the wine and the waiter filled their glasses. When he had gone Greg raised his. "To us."

"No," she said, looking down at the table, avoiding his eyes. "It's got to be to you. And to me. That way, I don't know anything about you, Greg. Only rumours." He didn't answer and she thought, what's the point, anyway. If he talked to her would he be telling the truth? She felt she had lost her ability to trust. Her father was not being honest with her. Martin . . . She felt a wrench in her heart when she thought of what he had done, that nobody seemed to take seriously except her. Am I wrong, she wondered? Should I be more tolerant? She felt she could talk to Greg about Martin. And then she wondered if that was simply because Greg did not like him. A man

81

who does not like another man will be biased in his opinions.

"Tomorrow I have to see Martin," she said, fingering her soup spoon. "I promised my parents." She wanted to tell him Oliver Wingate had said he would break her father. She needed advice. At the same time she was loath to burden him with her problems. He had enough of his own.

"You can't win with the Martins of this world. Either you share them, or you walk away," he said.

She wondered if he was talking about his wife.

"Anyway," he added lightly, "sometimes you look at someone and find you're cured. Maybe this will happen to you."

Again she wondered if he was referring to his wife who may or may not be dead. She looked at him helplessly. "Did you love her very much? Your wife?"

"Very much," he said.

We have our separate problems, she thought. There is considerable danger in two troubled people coming together for comfort.

"Let's dance," he said.

She stood up. As he put his arms round her she felt again that mysterious charge she had felt at the dinner in Positano. A subterranean thing. She smiled up at him and he smiled back.

The fathers had already been at work. Julie could tell by the lack of surprise in Martin's voice when she telephoned the next morning. But his pleasure sounded genuine. "I'll pick you up at noon and bring you back here to lunch."

"No, Martin." They had to meet on neutral ground, not at his parents' hotel. "Let's go to some quiet place where we can talk. Or better still, we could pick up sandwiches and go to Kensington Gardens."

Martin laughed softly. "Darling, what a sweet thought. But a bit ridiculous, don't you think? Sandwiches on a park bench?"

She flushed. They had had picnics by the Thames beneath

82

willow trees, and once in a field of corn, but there had always been a hamper and champagne.

She waited for him in the foyer, wearing a suit made by Moira in Paris. It had been intended as her going away suit after the wedding, but Martin was not to know that. There was a certain perversity in her choosing to wear it today. She wore strappy, high-heeled shoes. Long legs, long fair hair, she thought as she passed the desk looking down at her short skirt and high heels to avoid the curious eyes of the clerk. Why can't I get those two women I overheard in Positano out of my mind?

Then Martin swept up in his low, fast and glamorous Porsche five minutes late. She spun through the swing doors. He leapt out before she could open the door. "You shouldn't have waited on the pavement, darling, sweet girl. Don't you look gorgeous!" He kissed her on the cheek and settled her into the passenger seat then sauntered back round the bonnet with a swing in his step. "I've got a very secluded table tucked away in a bow window in a Soho restaurant," he said, taking her hand, then releasing it in order to change gear. They swept into the main stream of traffic that was headed for the West End.

The table was indeed secluded, cut off by a shelf of hors d'oeuvres from the small dining-room where tables were wedged together like pieces on a draughts-board. The head-waiter came to ensure they were comfortable and at ease.

Martin said, reaching across the table for her hands, "I've ordered champagne."

"This isn't a celebration. It's a talk. Please, Martin," she begged.

He took her engagement ring out of his pocket. "Let me put this back on your finger."

"No, Martin. I am no longer engaged to you." She withdrew her hands.

"Please. I can't enjoy my lunch until you do." He smiled at her in that winning way he had, reaching again for her hands. "Come on, darling Julie. Let me put it on."

"No. Martin, I want to talk about our fathers."

He said brusquely, "I will not talk about them. This is our life. They can stick to theirs."

"Like it or not, we're involved."

"We'll get out of it," he said, sounding as though the getting out would be the easiest thing in the world. He whispered, "Jul-ie, the ring. Your hand please. Come on, we're not going to get anywhere until I have this ring back on your finger." He reached across the table again and captured her left hand. Drew it towards him. Slipped the ring on. The beautiful stone shone in the light from the window. She remembered Greg saying, 'You can't win with the Martins of this world.' She felt herself losing. Felt she was stuck with the ring, now. She wished she hadn't come.

"Cancel the champagne," she said. She didn't want the trouble that would arise when she refused to drink. Didn't want him getting more and more relaxed, more and more amiable so that she could not fight him.

"Done."

Her heart jolted as she glimpsed the old Martin who had made her fall in love with him. Greg had said, 'Either you share people like Samantha and Martin, or you walk away.' She wasn't walking away. Here she was, in a public place, with his ring back on her finger. She sensed Antonia hovering.

"Duck paté," said Martin looking down at the menu, taking charge. "You'll let me order for you, won't you, darling?"

"You may as well."

He ignored her defeated tone. "Serbian chicken to follow. That's a speciality of the house."

"Martin, your father has threatened to ruin mine."

His head came up. He thumped the menu down on the table, looking outraged. "What balderdash! They've just settled their differences. They're the greatest friends. And besides, Julie my darling," he leant across the table, bringing his face and his shining eyes close, "we're not talking about parents. We're here to talk about us."

"It wasn't what I came for."

84

"It was what I came for, sweet girl," he said firmly. He looked back at the menu. "Serbian chicken comes with peppers and a fiery and aromatic sauce, that's what it says. You'll love it, my darling."

He was so tender. So affectionate. And so determined to win. She wanted to hit him over the head with a plate.

The waiter was hovering. Martin ordered. "And the house wine?" He looked across at Julie, asking with great courtesy. "A glass of the house wine?"

"All right," she said, immediately regretting the ungracious words. Martin was being so nice. She smiled at him, tentatively. The waiter signalled to the wine waiter. Martin looked down the list. Chose carefully. She wanted to say, 'You don't have to choose if you're ordering the house wine.' But she couldn't. Martin was going to win.

After they had finished, and the wine had been drunk, after the waiter had left them with coffee Martin reached across the table and held her hands. "Now, let's talk about us."

"'Us' is about our parents, you know that."

"No!" He slapped his hand down, palm first, on the table. "We're adults. This is our marriage. Ours."

"It's only ours if we go away by ourselves, Martin. If we don't take anything from our fathers," she pointed out.

"What on earth do you mean?" he asked defensively.

"It's too late. That's what I mean. We've allowed ourselves to be used. It didn't matter at the time that it suited them for us to marry. We wanted it, and it seemed wonderful for your father and mine to settle their differences. Now they've done it, we've got a responsibility, even though it was not of our own making."

"You weren't thinking of that when you walked out before the wedding, were you, little dove?" Martin's affection was honed now to a sharp edge.

"I didn't realise what tough businessmen our fathers are."

Martin broke in quickly. "We were talking about us, Julie. Not our parents. Let me repeat that – not our parents. There's no problem for them if we marry. That's what we've met to discuss. Our marriage. When are we going to get married?" He tried to grasp her hands.

"Have you told your father about your antiques business?"

"What antiques business?" He was bland. Innocent. At her incredulous gasp he smiled gently. "Surely that isn't still worrying you? Dear Julie, of course I've cancelled all that."

She asked suspiciously, "For good?"

"For the time being. There's no reason in the world why I shouldn't dabble in antiques when I've got the spare time. It's a dull fellow who is content with one job." He made it sound reasonable.

"That wasn't what you said before," she ventured uncertainly. "You said you weren't going into the hotel business at all."

"But I am. If that's all that's worrying you, darling love, I am. I've been convinced it's the right thing for us. Now, all we have to do is fix another date." He sat back in his chair, head lifted, his tawny eyes turning gold in the light. He squared his shoulders as though ready to take on the world with confidence. "What a storm in a teacup!"

He looked so relieved, so pleased with himself, that she thought with a stab of cold insight, 'I was one of his possessions, that's all. A possession! No more than a carriage clock, or a Ming vase he thought he had lost from his collection.'

"Let's go, shall we?"

Julie clasped her hands together tightly. "Martin, about Antonia . . ."

"Now, Julie. Forget the past." He looked irritably round the room. "Where has that waiter gone?"

"If it is the past . . ."

"Ah! There he is." Martin signalled. "Could we have the bill, please?"

86

"Martin, I said if it is the past . . ."

"Of course it is." He brushed her words aside like dust off a shelf. "For heaven's sake, Julie, you're like a dog with a bone. Everyone has an ex-girlfriend."

The waiter put a saucer down on the table. Martin picked up the folded paper from it, then put a wad of notes down.

"Come on, my love," he said.

"Martin!"

He was already rising.

"Martin, sit down again for a moment."

He opened the door. They were out in the street. Julie gripped Martin's arm, pulled him round so that he had to look at her. Swallowing her pride, she asked, "Martin, if I marry you, will I be the only one? I mean, the only woman in your life?"

"How could I make a promise like that?" he demanded, outraged. "It's the rest of my life you're talking about."

She felt cold, and oddly calm, because his deviousness was quite transparent. "I am talking about Antonia," she said. "I believe you love her very much, and that she loves you."

"You're talking about something you know nothing about," he said coldly. "I've promised to marry you."

She replied steadily, "It's not the answer I want."

"It's the one you've got. Can't you trust me?"

"No." She could not remember afterwards whether she had said it out loud or not before she turned and walked away, her footsteps quickening as she went, her high heels tap-tapping on the pavement.

"Julie!" She kept walking, hurrying, not looking where she was going. "Julie!" She crossed the road. Brakes screeched. A horn blared. A voice cried angrily. "Can't yer look where yer going?" She blinked, saw a taxi driver leaning out of his cab window, red-faced with fright.

"I'm sorry," she muttered. Then she saw his cab was empty. "Could you take me to Kensington?"

"Hop in." She struggled with the door and fell into the

back seat. "You're safer in my cab than out on the road," said the taxi driver forgivingly. "Cor, you didn't half give me a fright."

Chapter Six

At the Hotel Gideon a message was waiting for Julie – *'Your father has been called to Paris and your mother went with him. She said to tell you she would ring you immediately they arrive at the Hôtel Le Sceptre.'*

Julie heaved a sigh of relief. That, at least, meant another confrontation with her parents was postponed. She went upstairs and changed into working gear, a slim-fitting nut-brown skirt that came to well below her knees and tailored blouse.

Dan was in her office. He looked up as she entered. "How did things go?"

"I've got to decide whether to laugh or cry," she said. She pushed the light, bouncy hair back from her face, and her mouth turned down at the corners.

"It's bad, then?"

That now familiar lump thickened in her throat. "He's not going to give up Antonia, Dan."

"Did he say so?"

"No. But, in my heart, I know."

"Poor Julie."

Laugh or cry – she choked between the two. Dan waited while she shuffled papers on her desk, pretending to examine them. "The combination of problems is a little too strong for me." She made a half-hearted effort to smile. "Hurt pride; the possibility of my father losing his temper and being dreadfully angry; the guilt of taking Martin from a woman who – I can't help remembering all the time what you said. That there's something special about the relationship between Antonia and Martin." And she could not help remembering what Greg had said – that you can't win with that sort of person. You either share them, or walk away. She had walked away.

Dan gave her a sympathetic look. "I'll be here if you need me," he said, preparing to leave. At the door he turned. "By the way, how did you get on last night?"

She smiled ruefully. "My father saw Greg, realised he was with me, and got the wrong impression."

"I hope it remains the wrong impression," said Dan gravely. "I don't want you to think I'm interfering in your life, but to use a well-worn cliché, I would not like to see you step out of the frying pan into the fire."

She did not know what made her react so violently. Perhaps the wine Martin had insisted on having at lunch. "You *are* interfering," she said.

He closed the door and came back to stand by the desk. "Somebody has to help you, Julie," he said. "Strathallan isn't going to provide any answers. He's in a lot more trouble than you are. Is that what attracts you to him? A fellow feeling? If it is, pause before it's too late. You can't help him and I doubt if he can help you."

"That's where you're wrong," Julie said with a depth of feeling that surprised even herself and brought concern to Dan's eyes. "He can help me – and has. He's wise and kind. I feel lost, Dan. I've got no one to turn to."

He replied drily, "I'm doing my best."

"You're wonderful," Julie cried, "but—"

"I'm too perceptive, aren't I?" asked Dan shrewdly. "I know you so well now. Stop hesitating, Julie. Make a decision."

Yes. That was what she had to do. She looked up at him, clear-eyed, but with pain in her heart as well as fear of what her decision entailed. "I am not going to marry Martin. Not now, or ever." She added bleakly, because Dan was a friend of Antonia and must wish her well. "That should please you."

Dan didn't answer. But neither did he go. He stood where he was and she wondered if he was waiting for her to burst into tears. "Don't be bitter," he said.

"And don't get involved with Greg Strathallan. Is that what you're going to say next?"

"Out of loneliness," he said. "For the wrong reasons."

"And don't upset my parents."

He put an arm round her shoulders. The pressure was comforting. She kissed the back of his hand. Then he went out and closed the door behind him. Julie felt a tear roll down her cheek. She took a tissue from her pocket and wiped it away then pulled some papers towards her and picked up a pen.

Her mother telephoned. There were problems at Le Sceptre. Their manager's wife was ill and the head chef was threatening to leave. "I don't want your father to have any more worries. He was most upset last night. He told me there was a man waiting for you in the foyer. Someone called—"

"Greg Strathallan, Mother."

"Julie, don't be like that." Delia sounded upset. "You know we only have your interests at heart."

Not only mine, Julie thought and felt her heart harden. "And yes, if you're going to tell me he has a reputation, I do know that. But as you know I have been very unhappy and he has been kind to me."

There was a startled silence. Julie had a feeling her mother was having trouble coming to terms with the new woman she had become. "Now, about Martin. I did see him yesterday."

"There now. I'm so glad. With you two married, your father will be able to relax. He needs to let go of work problems at his age. Martin is young and strong."

"I can't marry Martin, Mother. I'm sorry." How many times was she going to have to say this before her parents were convinced?

There was another startled silence. "You told him that?"

"He won't give up Antonia."

"I don't understand this." Delia sounded bewildered. "Oliver told Neil categorically there had never been anything serious between Antonia and Martin. It's you he wants to marry, Julie. He loves you, only you, darling."

Julie heaved a sharp sigh.

"Martin *does* love you, Julie."

"I think he does in his own way. I'm just sorry I can't accept only a part of him."

"This will really upset your father!"

"Tell him I cannot marry Martin. Not even for him."

Delia said in a frightened voice, "You're in love with this other man!"

"No, of course not – oh, Mother, please try to understand how I feel. I don't want to let you and Father down, but I cannot – simply cannot . . ."

There was a click at the other end. Resignedly, Julie put the receiver down, wondered if she should ring back, decided against it, at least until she felt calmer. She was due for a day or two off. She decided to ask Dan if she could go to Paris at the weekend. She went in search of him and found him booking in guests. "Where's Miranda?" Miranda was the desk clerk who was supposed to be on duty.

Dan shrugged. "I found the desk unattended and these people waiting. Would you like to give me a hand?"

She called a porter, took over Registration and handed out the room keys. When the work was done and they were alone Dan said, "When you were on the phone to your mother Strathallan called. He waited a while, then hung up."

"Did he leave a number?"

"No. Actually, I didn't ask him." Dan looked down at the desk, shoulders hunched.

She picked up the receiver and dialled Directory Enquiries. Dan looked at her sharply. "You see, he told me the name of his firm." She wrote the number down, then handed the receiver to Dan. "Do me one more kindness, Dan. Ring this number for me."

He shook his head. "I won't be a party to your foolishness."

"Please, Dan. Their girl on the switch-board is going to ask who wants to speak to Mr Strathallan. I don't want to give my name. Please."

"I wish I hadn't told you now." But in his quiet, kindly way Dan took the receiver and dialled.

If Greg was surprised at her calling him he did not allow it to show. "How nice of you," he said. "I was merely checking to see if you need cheering up."

"As a matter of fact, I do." She heard the smile in her voice.

"Would seven be too early to call for you?"

"One moment." She checked with Dan. "Will I be free at seven? My own work is finished. Is there anything you'd like me to help with?"

Resigned, Dan shook his head. "I wish I could say yes in all honesty."

She spoke confidently into the receiver, smiling at Dan. "Seven would do very well."

"You're a fool, Julie," said Dan again as she replaced the receiver.

"Maybe I am."

She started to cross the foyer then turned. "If we're not busy at the weekend could I have a day or maybe two days off and dash over to have a talk with my parents. They're angry." She told him Delia had hung up on her.

Dan looked down at the bookings. "Yes, I think so. You're due for time off."

"Thanks."

This time she had no intention of waiting in the street for Greg. A kind of happy defiance had taken her in its grip and she did not care if there was staff gossip. She saw being seen with Greg as a hardening of her break with Martin. She went to her room and spent some time getting herself ready. She looked up to see Dan standing in the half open doorway to her room, surveying her, his eyes critical. "She brushed her golden hair until it shone," he said in that slow, contemplative way he had, then sliding his eyes downwards, "and wore her prettiest dress and a very unworking-girl necklace and a ring. Where did the ring come from, Julie?"

"Dan!" She rushed at him, gave him a playful push, laughing.

"It's true, though, isn't it?"

She said defensively, "I was getting married, remember? I had a lot of good clothes for the honeymoon. It's customary. What am I supposed to do with them? Fold them up in moth balls? And the ring is one my mother gave me for my 21st birthday.

He turned away. "Strathallan is waiting downstairs. That's what I came to tell you."

She picked up her mohair wrap and bag with the gold clasp. "Dan, you've been wonderful. I'll never forget how kind."

"OK. Then don't make a mess of things, that's all I ask in return. We good Samaritans don't like to see our good work go for nothing."

"I'll try not to." She squeezed his arm affectionately as they went along the passage towards the top of the stairs. "How did you know about Greg's troubles, Dan?"

"It was all in the papers. You were in Paris at the time. When he came here to eat, I recognised him from his photograph. He's married, Julie. Or else, if his wife is really dead and they never find her body . . ."

"Yes?" She waited, eyes bright, daring him to say it.

"Julie, he's never going to be free. You've got enough trouble on your hands. I'm fond of you. That's why I warned you about Antonia. Now this!"

She said briskly, "You'd prefer I didn't marry Martin because he's Antonia's property and you don't want me to be comforted by Greg. What do you want of me, Dan?"

He looked at her for a long moment. "If I thought there was the slightest chance of it happening, I'd say I would like you to marry me. But I'm too safe, aren't I, Julie? I'm the brother you didn't have. That's why you came to me when you didn't want to go home, wasn't it? Girls don't marry their brothers."

"Oh Dan!" She put out her hands and he took them. "You were never in love with me."

"I've never known you well. But I have really got to know you since you've been working here. Just let me say this, Julie dear, if you come a cropper, think

94

of me as a safety net. It doesn't sound romantic, but you don't see me as romantic, do you?" And without waiting for a reply he added, sounding wry and forlorn, "But you won't. You'll find another guy who'll treat you badly. You're that kind of girl. Is it the excitement you need?"

Julie laughed softly. "Darling Dan. I can't tell you what this talk has done for my morale. It sounds corny, but d'you know that old song 'I'm only a bird in a gilded cage?'"

He nodded.

"It occurs to me that's me. I've been tied to my family's business for so long that I had grown accustomed to owning the hotels and being owned by the family. I think I suddenly saw someone had left the cage door open. I'm establishing my independence."

"Caged birds that get away usually get eaten by bigger birds," Dan said. He took her arm. "Come on, let's walk downstairs. I'd like to think Strathallan has got tired of waiting but I don't expect he has."

Greg was standing, hands in pockets, watching the lift doors. Poised, Julie thought, like an eagle with wings lifting ready for take-off. He could not have heard them approach for their footsteps were silent on the thick stair carpet, but as though he sensed their coming his head turned. His face was still and then life flooded into it and he came forward smiling.

Dan greeted him courteously and saw them to the door. "Have fun."

"He's not sure you're in good hands," said Greg, smiling down at her, as though criticism to him was like water off a duck's back.

"He's a very good friend," she said.

"We all need those." But he said it lightly, impersonally, as though he himself had no problems.

It was a clear, cool evening. They sped out of town. Greg said he had booked a table at a restaurant by the river near Chiswick. The newly crisp autumn days had begun to turn the virginia creeper red. It drooped like possums' tails across the windows of the old Queen Anne house that had been converted to a restaurant. Inside, lamps glowed within red shades, lighting up the little white tables with their shining silver.

The head-waiter, frowning, was glancing worriedly down his list of bookings as they came to the door. He greeted them apologetically. "I'm very sorry, Mr Strathallan. We're fully booked."

"Farringdon," said Greg. "A Mr Farringdon booked for me. You've got that all right?"

"Farringdon? Yes." But he gave Greg a very odd look as he ticked off the name. As they sat down, Greg said, "You're wondering who Farringdon is."

"No. I mean – er – is he a friend of yours?" It was out of character for Greg to masquerade under an alias. And pointless, since clearly he was known here.

"People can be very intrusive," said Greg. "And I wanted you to have a nice evening."

"That's very kind." But she was puzzled. He took the menu and handed it to her.

"Don't feel obliged to tell me what occurred over lunch," he remarked offhandedly, giving the menu his full attention. "You're not on your own. Everyone has a rough patch in his life, remember that. Now, what are you going to eat?"

He was right, of course, not to discuss their troubles, Julie thought. As the evening rolled past turtle soup, a piquant *coq-au-vin* and into some delectable frozen pudding dripping sweetly with almond liqueur, she said to herself: 'If I'm worried about his booking the table in a false name, then I should not be here.' But she felt edgy. As though something was going to happen.

As they sipped their coffee, a man appeared quietly and stood looking down at them. They both became aware of his close proximity and glanced up. "What is it?" Greg asked.

And then, to Julie's dismay, the man flicked a Press card before Greg, then took a notebook from his pocket.

96

He said, "I understand your wife's friend has been interviewed in Brazil, Mr Strathallan, and said that she failed to turn up as arranged. Have you anything to say?"

Greg's face seemed momentarily to crumple, then it hardened and his eyes blazed in a dark face suddenly alight in the white glare of a photographer's flashlight.

So that was why Greg had booked the table in a false name! Julie gasped and both hands came up automatically to cover her face. The man saw the ring she was wearing, a small ruby her mother had given her, and asked, "Did Mr Strathallan give you that?"

Greg pushed back his chair. "Get out of here before I knock you cold."

The head-waiter hurried forward. "Mr Strathallan!"

"And as for you," Greg said witheringly, "this is the last time you get my custom." He picked up Julie's stole. "Get out of the way." He stood tall, a very angry man, towering head and shoulders over them.

"I d-didn't—" began the waiter, stuttering in abject confusion.

"Someone did." The other diners had stopped eating to stare. A sibilant whispering echoed round the room. Greg took Julie's arm and pulled her to her feet. "Come on."

The reporter stood his ground, attempting to bar the way. "Are you going back to Italy, Mr Strathallan? I understand the Italian police want to talk to you about finding your wife's car."

Greg pushed him aside so that the man had to grab at a table for support. The diners began to protest. At the door the manager was waiting. Greg dismissed him with a contemptuous nod. "Send me the bill, and don't expect a tip," he snapped. "I'm sure you'll have no trouble getting the address."

The reporter followed them into the car park. "Mr Strathallan, the police—"

"Get out of my way," Greg said curtly.

"I'm only doing my job."

"Then do it in future with a little more tact and perhaps you'll have some luck."

Shattered, Julie huddled in the passenger seat. Greg slid in behind the wheel. The engine burst into life and, as the car leapt forward, the reporter jumped aside.

They roared into the street, swung away from the river and headed for the London road. "I'm sorry," Greg said as he braked at the traffic lights. Then, remorsefully, "I've only myself to blame. I ought to have known, human nature being what it is, that I wouldn't get away with it."

Well, she could not say she hadn't been warned. "I suppose it's publicity for the restaurant."

"And no doubt his paper pays a fee to informers." Greg was still angry. "I'm sorry, Julie. Can you imagine what they're going to write, now they can bracket us together? I'm sorry to involve you. I tried so hard not to."

She was frightened but she made her voice light. "*Strathallan dining à deux with the blonde ex-girlfriend of Martin Wingate—*"

Greg broke in, "*Only hours after the news came through that his wife . . .* Yes, Julie, it was reported in tonight's paper. Sam did not turn up in South America, it seems. And now her car has been found in a lock-up garage in Amalfi."

The lights changed and the car forged ahead once more. "I'm sorry. I did what seemed at the time best for both of us – providing no one caught up with me. It came unstuck. What can I say except that I'm sorry?"

"I'm sorry, too." She hunched lower in the seat. "I mean, I'm sorry about you. It really doesn't matter about me. I'm going to Paris at the weekend to try to work out something with my parents. I'll be out of the reporters' way."

He did not need to know about her meeting with Martin. He seemed never to have taken her engagement seriously. Only the break with her parents bothered him.

There was not much traffic. They swept past green lights for most of the way. At the Gideon she said as he switched off the engine, "You must come in. I'll get you a whisky. Or coffee, if you'd prefer. The place will be almost deserted at this time."

He held her hand, his eyes thoughtful. "I think not, in the circumstances, thank you all the same. I'll see you inside though."

The hall porter was tidying up some fallen flower heads from the big bowl just inside the door. He looked up in relief as she came through, and hurried towards them. "Miss Creighton! A call came for you just after you left."

"Was it important?"

"Your father has been taken to hospital. You're to ring Paris immediately."

Julie stared at him, stunned. Then she felt Greg's hand slide firmly through her arm. Heard him ask quietly, "What has happened?"

"A heart attack, sir." Then, turning back to Julie, "Mr Barlow has been on to Heathrow. He's made a booking for 0640."

The whole world seemed to crash round Julie's head, guilt lying uppermost. I've done this to him, she thought. Speechless with emotion, she clapped a hand to either side of her face and closed her eyes.

"Julie." Greg's voice was gentle.

The porter's words came again, through the haze of despair. "Your mother is at the hospital; he's in intensive care. Shall I get the number for you, Miss Creighton?"

Weak at the knees, Julie made her way into Dan's office behind Reception. Greg's appearance at the Merrion last night must have been the final straw for her father.

Her mother was very upset when she came to the telephone. "Yes, yes, it is serious."

"Is he – is he—"

"We don't know yet. Darling, can you come over? It would help to have you here."

"Yes. Yes, of course. I'll be there as soon as I can, Mother."

A warm hand closed comfortingly on her shoulder. She spun round, wild with grief. "I've done this to him. I've upset him so much by refusing to marry Martin—"

"No one has any right," said Greg, "to tell us what to do with our lives."

Her eyes were enormous with fear. "That's all very well but I may have killed him. What am I going to do?" she cried.

"You're coming with me to sit quietly in a corner and have some coffee."

There were only one or two guests in the lounge. The single waiter who was still on duty was hovering close by, a white napkin over his wrist, silver tray in one hand. "Get some coffee for Miss Creighton, please." Greg led her to a big, comfortable sofa in the far corner. She no longer wanted to drive him away.

The waiter lifted a low table and placed it in front of them. She sat staring at it, numb with misery. "It's my fault. It's my fault."

"If apportioning blame is going to make you feel any better, I'd suggest you might consider it's Martin Wingate's fault for making it impossible for you to marry him," said Greg crisply.

They sat in silence. Greg seemed to understand she was too devastated to talk. After a while the waiter came back with a pot of coffee and two cups on a silver tray. "Is there anything else, Miss Creighton?"

"No, I don't think so, thank you."

"Mr Barlow has ordered a mini-cab for a quarter-to-five in the morning. Will that suit you?"

"Don't bother," said Greg. "I'll drive her to Heathrow."

She knew she should protest. She had no right to keep him up all night. The waiter was still hovering, waiting for her answer. Greg waved him away and he went reluctantly, still looking at Julie. The scene in the restaurant came flashing back to her. Did the waiter know Greg's identity? Did everyone know? Had further news of his wife's disappearance been reported in the evening papers? On the radio? There might possibly be reporters even now camped on his doorstep.

He said, "Drink up your coffee. Would you like a brandy?" She shook her head. "I'll leave you as soon as you've finished. There's time for a few hour's sleep. Try to sleep. Try not to blame yourself. It won't do your father any good. I'll be here at a quarter-to-five."

She packed everything, knowing she would not be returning to the Gideon. Miraculously, she did drift off to sleep, though intermittently, and was awake when the telephone rang by her bed.

"Four o'clock, Miss Creighton. There's a letter for you at reception from Mr Barlow. Will you pick it up as you go?"

"Thank you."

Outside, the early morning lay dark and still. She dressed swiftly in a warm coat and skirt with a thin polo-neck sweater, and wound her hair round her head.

The night porter brought her a cup of tea. "We'll miss you," he said. "I hope you find good news waiting for you in Paris."

"Thank you, Albert. You've all been very kind to me."

Greg was waiting in the foyer. She noticed immediately that he looked tired and strained; that he wore the same dark suit in which he had left at midnight. She exclaimed in consternation, "You haven't been home!"

He took her bag, and ushered her out of the door. "Never mind me," he said brusquely and she was reminded of that other Greg in Positano, looking down the companionway at her as she left his wife's cabin saying 'Don't you know port from starboard?'

He threw her bag into the car and opened the door for her.

"Greg, is something wrong?" It was not only that he appeared to have been up all night. He was tense, strained as tight as a violin string.

"Something will be wrong if we don't get you to Heathrow in time. Hop in."

She said in a small voice as he revved up the car, "You're being so good to me, but you're in trouble too. Won't you let me share?"

He turned on her a look she could not begin to understand, and then he seemed deliberately to shift his mood. "My shoulders are broad," he said, sounding laconic, but with something deeper, darker showing through.

He dropped her with her bag at the terminal. The sky was pale in the east. "Wait here. I'll park the car."

She began to protest but he was away again, out of sight round a corner in seconds. He seemed an interminable time. She began to wonder if something had gone wrong. Eventually he came running. "Sorry," he said breathlessly, "I had to go to the long-term car-park."

"Long-term? Why?"

"I'm going with you."

"Greg! No, you don't have to do that," she protested. Then she looked up into his face and saw with a feeling of inevitability that it was more than strained. It was haggard, and then she saw his suit was crumpled as though he may have slept those waiting hours in the car.

"Come on," he said, picking up her bag. "We're running short of time and I have to collect my ticket." He took her arm and hurried her along.

"But Greg, you don't have to come with me," she said again, thinking that his presence would not help with her family. "It's terribly kind of you and I do appreciate it but—"

He broke in tersely, "I'm going on to Naples."

All through the bustle and boredom of getting away, Greg was quiet but he was not calm. The tenseness stayed and his eyes were watchful, darting here and there as they made their slow way through Passport Control, the ticket check-point, the security search.

As they entered the departure lounge her glance stopped at the book stall with its piles of evening papers. She looked quickly away. Greg steered her to a seat. There was no privacy for talking, and besides, Greg did not seem to be in the mood. She took Dan's letter out of her handbag and read it.

'Dear Julie,' it ran, 'I'm deeply sorry about your father. I'll be in touch. I imagine this means you'll have to assume family responsibilities so don't worry if you feel you can't come back. I've been in touch with Vera Turnbull whom you replaced. Her mother is about to go into a hospice so she'll be able to resume her job quite soon.' He ended, 'With love, Dan.'

She folded the letter and slipped it back into her bag with a feeling of relief. She closed her mind and tried not to think at all. Waiting for boarding time seemed interminable but it came at last. As they fastened their seat-belts and the plane began to creep along the tarmac, Julie heaved an enormous sigh of relief.

He looked down at her and his face relaxed. "Thanks for being so patient."

For not asking questions? She had been afraid to ask. Now she murmured, "The reporters were waiting for you at your flat?"

"No," he replied soberly. "The police." At first she did not properly take it in. Then he said, "I saw their car outside, so I kept going."

"You – you're running away?" She could not believe it. Greg running!

"I'm flattered by your surprise," he told her drily. "Let's say I'm perfectly capable of getting to Naples under my own steam. It's really no concern of the English police. Also, I'm very much afraid Samantha did meet with an accident. Alive or dead, she must be found, now."

"I wish I could come with you. I wish you weren't so alone."

He took her hand in his. "I wish it could have been different," he said.

In France, with Paris awakening, Greg put her into a taxi. "Good luck," he said. "I do hope your father will be all right."

"And good luck to you." She felt an overwhelming sorrow for him. She waved until the cab shot into a double traffic lane and Greg disappeared behind the hurrying cars. Then she sat back in her seat.

She wished she had kissed him. She wondered why he had not kissed her. It would have been a natural, friendly gesture in view of his kindness. Yet she knew with a deep, internal hunger, that natural and friendly were dull words, that did not belong in the context of their relationship any more. That kisses between them now would, inevitably, be more than that.

Chapter Seven

The well-loved head on the pillow was still, the eyes closed. Her mother's relief as Julie came into the room was enormous. She rose from the bedside, kissed her, and for a moment they clung together.

"He's better," she whispered. "It was the worry and upset. First you, then the staff trouble at the hotel."

"What staff trouble?"

"Oh Julie, I don't want to go into that now. It all caught up with him. Be careful what you say, my dear. It's crucial that he be kept calm."

"Yes, of course." Julie retreated into silence, swallowing her resentment that her mother's greeting had been a placing of blame. Delia's eyes were swollen, her face set into deep lines of strain. She looked desperately tired. She went to the bed and stood looking down at her father. She kissed him very lightly on the forehead. He did not stir. She turned back to her mother. "If there's somewhere for you to lie down I'll hold the fort. You've been up all night, haven't you?"

Delia's mouth trembled. "I couldn't get hold of you. Where were you?"

"I'm sorry. I went out to dinner."

"With Martin?"

She looked into her mother's eyes, saw the fear and the intense hope, and turned away. "We had a lot to talk about," she said. Sometimes you had to distort the truth. At least she was exercising compassion.

"It would make such a difference if your father's mind was at rest about the business," Delia whispered.

"Yes. You must have a sleep, Mother. I'll call you if there's any change."

105

The nurse, returning, heard her words. "Come with me, Mrs Creighton."

It was hot in the room so Julie removed her coat and laid it across the end of the hard white bed. Her father looked peaceful lying there on his pillows but his colour was bad.

She stood looking down at him, feeling love and regret in equal parts. She put a tender hand lightly over his. He opened his eyes and she started guiltily. "I'm sorry. I've wakened you."

"No. I sensed you were there. They brought you over from London. Am I that bad?"

"You're not bad at all. You're on the mend now. But you gave us a scare."

His gaze roved round the room.

"Mother has gone to have a rest. She's been up all night, keeping you company."

"Yes. I was hoping . . ." His eyes were troubled. "Martin's not with you?"

She shook her head. "I'll call him – later."

Her father gazed worriedly up into her face.

Julie thought with deep distress, I am not myself any more. I am their chattel. I have to marry Martin or my father will die. This is what they have decided.

"We'll work something out," she said and wondered grimly if it would prove to be the truth.

He moved his hand, touched her fingers. "You're all your mother and I have, Julie."

Julie forced herself to smile. "Sure. Me and a handful of old hotels. Now make certain you get better, because you're the only father I have." She leaned over and kissed him.

The nurse came gliding back on her soft-heeled shoes. "Mr Creighton," she scolded, "you should not be talking."

He said, clinging to Julie's hand as though she alone could save him. "This is my daughter. Isn't she pretty?"

The nurse waved Julie away. "I'm pretty too, and I'm the one you're stuck with," she said briskly. Julie smiled and backed into a chair. The nurse took the patient's wrist in one hand, her watch in the other, frowning.

Then, replacing his hand on the bedcover, she said, "The

doctor is on his way. I'm going to ask your daughter to leave." Outside the room she said quietly, "Your father is gravely ill, Miss Creighton. Your presence seems to have disturbed him. His pulse rate is up. I think it would be better if you leave him to us."

"Yes. Of course. But I promised Mother I would stay."

"I'm in charge here and I decide who will stay," the nurse replied bossily. "I'm sure your mother will understand that." She gave Julie a critical, searching look. "If there's anything you can do to set your father's mind at rest, I'd advise you to do it."

So Delia, thrown off balance no doubt by the shock of her husband's attack, had been telling her troubles to the nursing staff. Julie tried to understand. Alone, in the same circumstances, might not she have done likewise? But all the same, the nurse had no right to blackmail her.

Outside, an unseasonal wind was whipping a few tangled early autumn leaves along the pavement. Julie felt tired and upset by the lack of sleep as well as the strain. Her head had begun to ache. A taxi pulled in to unload a florist's messenger laden with bouquets for the hospital. On an impulse she engaged it and gave the name of Moira's boutique. Julie had many friends in Paris whom she could have visited. People, though, who knew Martin, or had at least met him, if only at the engagement party. At least Moira's views should be dispassionate on that score.

Moira saw her come through the door and ran forward. "Julie! *Cherie!*" She flung her arms round Julie in an extravagant show of affection. "And no suntan!" she cried in mock horror. "You borrow my villa in the sun and you dare to return without a tan!"

The doorbell tinkled and one of those extraordinarily elegant women, who always seemed to find their way to Moira's, strolled in.

"Violette!" Moira called imperiously in French to one of her staff. "Please to attend to Madame." Then, turning warm-heartedly back to Julie, "You will sit down beside me at my desk and we will pretend, for the clients, to be engrossed in business. Sit here and tell me what has happened now." She looked warmly into Julie's face, "Why, you are so pale! You are not well, *ma chérie*! Tell me everything."

Everything? The dark despair? The hopelessness? No, not that.

They went to the rear of the salon and Moira settled, as she had suggested, at a little antique desk. Julie took a low chair facing the window with her back to the room. Out in the courtyard there was a fountain and tubs full of flowering plants. Behind them, clients coming and going kept up a constant drift of chatter. She told Moira why she was back in Paris.

"You have given your father a heart attack simply by appearing with the wrong man? Rubbish!" said Moira vigorously, refuting the guilt.

Julie said, "Even I have to admit it could contribute to his stress."

"But what were you doing with Greg? I ask you, Julie! Greg is in trouble. You are in trouble. Two disasters do not make one success. Oh dear!" Moira jerked back in her chair, closed her eyes, banged both slender fists on the table. "Some of the blame must be on me. It really did not occur to me when I offered you the villa that Greg would appear."

"What did you mean by that enigmatic telegram? I asked you before but you side-stepped."

Moira was thoughtful. Then she said, "Julie, Greg is a friend of mine. And so are you. How can I telegraph you saying—" She shrugged and lifted her hands in that expressive way she had. "One does not go into explanations by telegram. I give a little advice and hope you will exercise your own discretion. Nor does one talk by telephone. You are going to ask me next why I didn't answer your call. That is why. Now, because we are talking confidentially I can say this. Keep away from him, Julie. Did you know they have discovered Samantha did not go to Brazil after all?"

Julie nodded. "What sort of person was Samantha?"

"Lovely. Awful. A wonderful, crazy, chameleon person. Greg has always attracted that kind of woman. Perhaps because of his looks? His wealth? He's smooth and tough and he enjoys their company. They don't get under his skin. But Samantha did. I never saw a man behave so out of character when she turned up. She could make him do anything! And she did – just for the sake of it, I sometimes thought. He even sold his racing yacht and bought that ridiculous gin palace of a cruiser because she wouldn't go out in *Sea Tiger*."

"Why?"

"*Sea Tiger* was a man's boat," said Moira. "It wasn't nearly comfortable enough for Samantha. He bought *Neptuna* as a wedding present for her. And then what did she do?" Moira asked the rhetorical question looking into Julie's eyes.

Compulsively, Julie needed to know every side of this matter. "What, Moira?"

"Oh, she was such a bad wife, that girl. And Greg was so good to her. She wasn't worthy of him in any way. She killed his love for her, in the end. Greg is tough, but he's a good man. Even when he must have realised he had a bad wife he tried his hardest to make the marriage work. But Sam was a natural cheat. She got her excitements from hurting people, even those she loved. She was beastly to her parents. And yet they have turned against Greg.

"Somehow, that's a part of what had to happen. When you have a daughter like Sam, even though you may love her dearly, you must live with the possibility that one day she might tease the wrong person, drive someone to distraction. They know Greg is not a man to cross. They may have thought he would tame her, and, when he didn't well . . ." Moira shrugged. "People who don't really know him, as Samantha's parents didn't, might think anything. Julie, I'm serious. Promise me you will stay out of Greg's way at least until this business has been cleared up."

"Surely, when people are in trouble, that's when they need their friends. I thought he was a friend of yours."

"Oh, Julie, Julie. When you look at me like that with those great, big, haunted eyes you scare me. Of course Greg's a friend of mine. And I'm very fond of him. But there is quite enough on your plate. You must not get involved in that mess."

Her insistence was so emphatic it jolted a chord in Julie's memory. Her lashes drifted down, hiding her tell-tale expression of apprehension. "Was Samantha tall with long legs, neat features, and long blonde hair?"

"Yes. You've seen a picture of her, then?"

With a nervous movement Julie jumped up. "I've wasted enough of your time. It's been lovely seeing you. I've got to get back to Le Sceptre anyway, where Mother can get in touch with me if she needs to."

Moira rose, smoothing the heavy folds of her skirt over hips so fleshless they seemed merely to form a frame for the elegant silk. "I'm sorry about your father, Julie darling. If there's anything I can do . . ."

There was always plenty to do in a hotel for one who knew the ropes. Julie let herself into the penthouse suite with her own key. Her father's desk in his study was piled up with papers. She looked through them, then sent for Pierre, the deputy manager. Anatole, the manager, had gone home to be with his sick wife.

"I'll be working here while my father's in hospital," she said, speaking in French as she always did with the staff. "Perhaps you could put me in the picture with regard to what happened before Monsieur was taken ill. My mother said there were staff problems."

Pierre stood with hands clasped behind his back, a slim, dark-suited figure scarcely taller than herself, with black hair and a thin face. "The chef threatened to leave. There was a scene. He recognises that he is not without blame for what has happened to Monsieur, and he has agreed to stay, at least until it is seen whether the matter can be sorted out. It is a personality problem. Leon feels he is being usurped by his new assistant who has the ear of your father. He was recommended most highly, you understand, by Mr Wingate." Pierre said pointedly.

Recommended by Martin's father? A needle of worry

110

pricked the back of Julie's mind. She frowned. There seemed to be an ominous note to Pierre's explanation.

Pierre's face softened. "Our hearts are all with you, M'selle." His meaning was all too clear. The French knew an arranged marriage when they saw one. He looked at her closely. "It won't make any difference to the staff? The amalgamation, I mean?"

"Why should it? The changes will be at a higher level." But even as she said it, she knew this was not entirely true. Pierre knew it, too. There had been changes already. Oliver Wingate had recommended a chef who did not fit in.

"I hadn't said anything to your father. I hoped he might bring up the subject himself, but he didn't. We're all worried."

"What is it, Pierre?" She tried to keep her own genuine concern out of her voice. It was not fair to allay his fears when she knew only too well they were valid.

"There is some question of changing staff around, M'selle, I mean, with staff from Mr Wingate's hotels. I'd like you to know I wouldn't wish to leave here."

She checked a very real feeling of apprehension, "I think you would find Mr Wingate an equally good employer."

"I would not like to go." His thin mouth grew thinner, his eyes more anxious.

She held her own anxiety in check. "I'll see my father understands."

"There may be other members of the staff who feel the same way. There are," he corrected himself.

It was a warning, she knew, and one she must not ignore.

She went through her father's files. There was little there that was unfamiliar to her. But what was this? A letter from Maurice Fouard, the manager of Hôtel le Bosquet in Geneva. She read it, frowning. It was in the form of a protest. Why had he not been consulted re refurbishment which anyway, in his view, was not necessary. He must know that the designs submitted were not at all suitable for an old style family hotel. Decoration along these lines would change its character radically.

Julie looked for a copy of a reply and failed to find one. She put the file away feeling very disturbed indeed.

Julie did not return to the hospital. Delia said the doctors insisted the patient should be kept quiet. Only she was allowed in. In a way, it was a relief. With her mother spending most of her time there, she and Julie met only in the evenings. Her mother was strained, often very tired.

Julie arranged for a bulletin on Neil's health to be left at the desk so that they would not be disturbed. Sometimes Delia ate at the hospital. When she came back to Le Sceptre she and Julie had dinner in the penthouse suite, for in spite of the bulletin there were always kind friends who wanted to come to their table and talk. Her mother came in from the bedroom wearing her outdoor clothes. She no longer had the energy or the will to dress up in one of her hostess gowns. Besides, sometimes when she had decided to stay at home she became fidgety and after a while went back to the hospital. Julie smiled at her and received a tired smile in return. She wished she could talk to her about the unrest among the staff. But Delia had never been encouraged by her father to take an interest and this was not the time to start.

This evening their dinner had been brought up. Delia sat down at the table and looked at the cold soup without interest. "Your father keeps asking about Martin. The cancellation of the wedding. It's on his mind."

Julie picked up her spoon and put it down again.

"I'm sure that's what's holding him back," Delia said.

Julie wanted to say, 'That's blackmail.' She held her anger in check. "I'm sorry," she said, "but I cannot marry Martin. I cannot keep on saying it. You must accept it. What is puzzling me is why it's so important to you. It very clearly is, yet neither of you have explained. I'm sure you know, Mother. I'm sure this is something that you do know about." She pushed her soup aside, rose and poured a glass of wine.

"I don't want a drink, dear."

Julie put the glass down beside her on the table. "It will do you good. Relax you." She poured another for herself. "We

112

really ought to talk." She smiled encouragingly at Delia. "Tell me what the problem is that will be solved by my marrying Martin."

"It would be to the advantage of all of us. And you. After all," she picked up her glass, raised it. "He is such a nice boy, Julie. Here's to both of you."

"And Antonia?" Julie's voice emerged hard as iron. "As this is to be a *ménage à trois* you may as well drink to her too."

"Now you're being silly." Delia returned to her soup. She didn't seem to have noticed that Julie was not eating. She took her mother's plate and put it aside. Reached into the hot cupboard and brought out a second course for her.

"What's this about Martin's father breaking him? Can you explain that?"

"He is afraid of what Oliver Wingate will do."

"How can he do anything, Mother?" Julie asked impatiently.

"I don't know. Neil hasn't explained the finer details to me," she added evasively. "You should talk to him about it."

"You said the sister-in-charge doesn't want me to visit him."

Delia flicked back her pretty greying hair. "That's true. She doesn't want him to talk business, or even think about it. But you can't stop a man thinking when he's worried."

Julie said. "You'll have to go along with him, just until he's well enough to know the truth. Some time he will have to recognise I can't marry Martin."

Delia looked at Julie with scared eyes. "I keep thinking about that man – Strathallan. Tell me about him, darling. Put my mind at rest."

'*Tell me you don't love him*' is what she means, Julie thought with that now familiar rush of panic. She swallowed hard, took a deep breath and produced a middle-of-the-road reply, "He's married, Mother."

"It's not much of an answer, darling. Not these days. Besides, in his circumstances, I mean, his wife . . ."

"What about his wife?" Julie looked steadily across the table at her mother, trying to hold her attention.

Delia cast around for a handkerchief, searching in her sleeve, her pockets. When she looked back at Julie she wore a defeated air. "We used to be able to talk to each other," she said.

"That was when I was more a daughter than a person in my own right. I've changed, and neither you nor Father have made any attempt to accept it. I don't want to talk to you about Greg."

"Why not?"

Julie shrugged. "You haven't met him. You don't know anything first hand about him."

Delia glanced down at the table. "You haven't eaten your supper," she said.

"You have," said Julie. "That's all that matters. Now, off you go to the hospital."

Her mother stood up, went to the door, hesitated. "Surely I'm entitled to know about this man."

"I think you know a fair bit. Possibly more than I do."

Delia looked taken aback.

"You've more time for gossip than I have."

"You're becoming unkind, Julie."

"Yes, well. Circumstances affect one." She softened and asked cautiously, "What do you want to know?"

"I'd like to know if you're going to see him again. Surely I am entitled to know, dear, considering the circumstances."

"He's gone to Italy."

Again she said, "That is no answer."

"We made no plans to meet."

Delia rested her arms on the back of the chair. "Are you saying you're not in touch with him?"

"Not at the moment."

Unbelievably, Delia breathed an enormous sigh of relief. She bent down and kissed Julie. "Why don't you come to the hospital with me?" she suggested impulsively. "That is, if you're willing to – as you say – put your father's mind at rest."

"Oh really, Mother!" Julie found herself laughing weakly.

114

"You'd better go. We're never going to get anywhere with this issue." She was astounded that Delia, who in normal situations was not very strong, could put up this impenetrable barrier to understanding. "And there's another thing. If he starts to ask questions about the hotel I'm going to have to change the subject. You see, Mother, this amalgamation is causing problems. The staff are afraid they may be moved round."

"Of course they'll be moved round, Julie. That's part of the plan."

"And you haven't told them? Has it occurred to you that people apply for jobs in Le Sceptre and the Merrion and Le Bosquet because they want to work for Father *not* the Wingates?"

Delia put a hand to her brow. "Julie, it's no use talking business to me. This is something for you and your father—"

"I'm not allowed to discuss business with my father. Remember?" It was like talking to a child.

"Oh Julie! I don't know what to do."

"All right, I'll be here with you. I'll telephone Dan. He's very understanding. He doesn't expect me to come back if I'm wanted here."

"You can stay? Oh, Julie, that's such a relief." All Delia's problems seemed to drop away. "I must go." She went swiftly to her room and returned with her coat. "Do please eat some dinner."

Julie nodded vaguely. She said as she helped her mother on with her coat, "I want to have a marriage like yours. Wouldn't you like that for me?"

"Of course. But you could have," Delia cried distractedly. "Martin is a lovely boy."

"Come on," said Julie bleakly. "I'll see you downstairs."

She put her mother into a taxi. As she re-entered the doors the desk clerk called, "M'selle. A call for you."

Fear came so easily. She felt it in the pit of her stomach. Without speaking, she signed that she would like the call transferred to her office. If her father was dead it would be her fault. Guilt spread through her, choking her. She stood

115

at the desk, muscles tensed, plucking up courage to lift the receiver.

A familiar voice said, "Julie. Hi."

She collapsed into her chair and began to laugh. Gratitude, pleasure, excitement rushed in to take the place of panic. "Greg! Oh, I am so pleased." Relieved, she meant, but she said pleased. The word jumped in. He seemed delighted but faintly puzzled. She explained. "Every time the phone rings I think it might be the hospital."

"How is your father?"

"Not well." Then she blurted out, "It's my fault. It seems I have to tell him I'll marry Martin before he'll get well." She hated herself for saying it. It seemed disloyal. But she had to lance the fear. She needed help. There was a moment's silence and she added, "I'm sorry. I shouldn't burden you with my troubles."

He ignored her apology. "Have you eaten?"

"No."

"Good. I'll pick you up in five minutes."

"You've got your car?"

"No. But I've borrowed a perfectly adequate Citroen from our Paris office. There's a nice little restaurant I know in the Bois."

"Great!" Then she asked diffidently, "Do you mind if I ask you to wait outside?"

He seemed to understand. "I intended to do that."

She sang as she danced into her bedroom and flung the wardrobe door back, shedding her blouse and undoing her skirt as she went. She snatched an elegant dinner dress from its hanger. The more she wore trousseau clothes the quicker they lost the stamp of their source. She drew some green eye-shadow carefully along her lids and smudged it evenly with the tip of her little finger, flicked some mascara on her lashes and touched her lips briefly with a dusky pink lipstick.

She brushed her hair high with extravagant, sweeping strokes and let it fall, shook it into a semblance of order and gave it a pat into place. Then she picked up a white woolly jacket and a small bag. In the hall she wrote a note to her mother. '*Gone out to dinner. Love, Julie.*'

Too late, she realised her mother would misunderstand. She would think Julie had known, when she did not eat the meal sent up for them, that she was going out. And with Greg. Who else? She couldn't think about it now. Greg would be waiting for her. She swung through the doors and there he was standing by a white car, smiling.

They swept down the Champs Elysées in a raging flood of evening traffic, the blues, reds, golds of the neon signs brazen in the soft black velvet of the night. Into the ordered whirlpool of the Place de L'Etoile and out, the big car lifting itself elegantly like a smug cat to race off towards Versailles. Julie laughed on the wind, hair flying.

The restaurant had once been a mill. It lay serene in a cloak of forest over a gushing stream. There were only half a dozen cars in the courtyard that was behind the main building, a secret, cobbled corner heavy with vines. She said with some satisfaction, "The reporters aren't going to find us here."

"It exists solely for people like us."

She smiled up at him thinking there are no people like us. Entrapped, yet in two different traps.

Inside, the tables were secret, too, divided by trellis and narrow window boxes bright with begonias. The lights were low, the tables candlelit. The waiter pulled out their chairs. They sat down facing each other. Greg handed her a menu and picked up the wine list. When they had ordered Greg looked at her across the table and said, "Your father's heart attack isn't about you, Julie. It's about Oliver Wingate."

"What makes you say that?"

"He's the hardest and one of the most unscrupulous men I know. The amalgamation of the hotels is an excellent thing business-wise, but Wingate is getting more out of it than your father."

That made sense, in view of what her father had said, that Oliver Wingate would break him if he didn't go through with it. She wondered if she should tell Greg, and decided against it, for the moment.

"You're looking for reasons why your parents want

117

you to marry Martin. Would you like me to hazard a guess?"

"Please do."

"Your father doesn't trust Wingate. He wants the amalgamation, but only on condition he's got you in there to keep an eye on things. And Wingate wants the amalgamation at all costs, because he knows he'll get control. He's the kind of chap who would think – Julie? She's only a girl. He would reckon he could walk over you."

"He couldn't," retorted Julie adamantly.

"If I read Martin correctly, he and his father together would be more than a match for you. Remember you're living with Martin—"

"I am not!"

Greg laughed and put his hand over hers on the table. "You're jumpy. I must choose my words more carefully. I'm looking at a hypothetical situation. As Martin's wife you've got to keep him happy. *Ipso facto*, you've got to give in to him if it suits him to go along with his father."

The waiter came with their starters. They sat in silence. Julie's mind was leaping and dancing, colliding with possibilities and probabilities. She felt invigorated by Greg's confidence. She hadn't realised to what extent, in spite of her surface fighting back, she had remained in her heart her parents' obedient and guilty daughter.

The waiter finished setting out the paté and went on his way. Greg tasted the wine, then the wine waiter left. He raised his glass. "To us, Julie. Us separately, if that's how you want it." He looked at her hard and a slow smile spread from the corners of his mouth. "But I wonder if you do, now?"

She said impulsively, pushing aside turbulent thoughts of his trip to Amalfi which she had yet to hear about, if he should choose to tell her; if she should dare to listen. "Let's drink to us."

"Skol."

"Skol." They smiled at each other.

"Let's start." He picked up his fork. "I don't know your father, Julie, only by repute. I understand he's one of the

118

old school. What used to be called a gentleman. Wingate eats that type for breakfast."

Julie felt cold. Now was the moment, without being disloyal, to tell Greg what her father had said.

Greg nodded. "True to type. But haven't you asked yourself why he's in a position to break him? Does your father owe him money?"

"Why should he?" Julie was defensive. But then, she realised something had got her father into Oliver Wingate's clutches. She couldn't rule out the fact that they owed him money. But why? "It's unlikely that my father will be back at work for some time. Perhaps never. If we owe money, then I shall have to pay it back. I'm in charge now."

"I'm amazed it didn't occur to you before." He raised one eyebrow, sardonically.

"You didn't know what a good daughter I was. That was the trip wire. I think I'm too much like my parents."

"Not ruthless enough," said Greg. "Not ruthless at all?"

"Probably not." She recognised that she might have sat her mother down, ignoring whimperings, tears, protests of loyalty, and demanded to know what was going on.

"Don't forget I'm here. The City is the place you look for money when you need it. I'm a City man."

"Thank you, Greg. I hope it won't come to that."

"Win or lose – no half measures," Greg said. "That's always been my motto. But keep it clean. There's the rub. It becomes difficult when other people ignore the rules."

Her eyes lifted to meet his and she felt his strength flow through her.

"Not that I'm advising you, or anyone, to emulate me," Greg added, looking nevertheless like a flag-flying winner – at the helm of his racing yacht *Sea Tiger* with the lost Samantha laughing at his side. The enigma of it came raging back, swamping Julie. Long legs, neat features, long blonde hair was how people had described Greg's wife. Samantha looked like her. She jumped as though an arrow had struck her.

"What's the matter? Someone walk over your grave?"

She said, "We're talking about my troubles. I haven't

119

asked you what happened in Italy. You don't have to tell me. I don't need to know. Only, it does one so much good to talk. Look at me!" She felt different. Knew she looked different.

"I don't want to burden you with it," Greg said. "You've enough on your plate. I'll sort it out."

"I know men don't like to talk about their troubles," she said, "but look where it landed my father."

He said reluctantly, "What the papers said was true."

"I didn't see them."

"They found Samantha's car. There was a villa with a garage in the rock below it. You know how they build them on the Amalfi coast. The villa had been empty all summer. I had often noticed the garage myself, with the door half-open. Then it was shut, and I assumed the owner had returned. But he only returned this week and reported the car to the police."

"What does it mean?" Even as she asked the question, she was remembering what Moira had said. That Samantha liked drama. That she liked to hurt people. Could hiding the car be a part of the game she was playing?

Greg said, "There's no explanation that I can see. She could have taken it to the airport and left it there until someone found it. Of course, hiding it in an empty garage in Amalfi and taking a taxi to the airport meant she was untraceable if her friends chose not to tell about her plans to go to South America."

"So what does it mean?" Julie asked again.

Greg glanced up, saw the waiter approaching and said briefly, "It could mean, if foul play was involved, that the guilty party wanted time to elapse before a hue and cry was set up."

The waiter came with their second course. They sat in silence until he had gone. When they were free to talk again Greg's mood seemed to have changed. "I don't want you involved," he said. "I don't intend to mess up your life, Julie."

"Don't you think it's pretty messed up already?"

"I hope I've helped with that." There was a finality about his tone.

120

She asked insistently, "What do you think happened to Samantha?"

"I think she may have met with an accident. Accidents happen to people all the time, especially around cliffs and boats. Especially, too, when they're guilty, in a hurry, nervous. She would have been all those things. But until or unless her body is found . . ." He made no attempt to finish the sentence.

"Greg!" She reached across the table and put her hand over his. "You're being loyal. And you're in trouble. You've gone a long way towards sorting me out tonight. You must let me help you. Please!"

He heaved an enormous sigh. "I don't think you can help me, Julie. No one can do that. I'm in this up to my neck and I'd hate to involve you. It's very unpleasant. It was nice of you not to read the papers, but perhaps you should have."

"I might not have found the truth there."

"You may have found the truth, but not the background."

"Let's have that, then, shall we?"

His mouth turned down. "When I married Samantha I knew about her relationships with other men, but I thought possession was nine points of the law. For people like Samantha, however, and perhaps Martin too, there is no law. She was like a child trying to see how far it can go with its parents before they react. She had to live with – well, a sort of danger. If you understand that, you may understand Martin. You can't win with such people. You either share them or you walk away. On a desert island, our marriage would have been a great success. But unfortunately there are very few desert islands left."

He pushed his plate aside and picked up his glass. His eyes were sardonic. "Bear in mind what I've told you when you go to see Martin and you may find yourself cured, and free."

"Is that what happened to you? Did you suddenly see clearly?"

His eyes were steady as he looked into hers. "When it was too late."

Her heart ached for him.

"Samantha was the spoiled only child of wealthy parents. She had only to lift a finger to get her own way. But having got it, she was delightful company. I hadn't intended to follow in her indulgent parents' footsteps, but I did, because I found it was the only way to get her to marry me, and after that the only way to live."

"What do you mean?"

"I hate to say this about someone who may be dead, but Samantha could make life hell if things didn't go her way." They waited again while the waiter fussed around, removing plates. When he had gone Greg asked, "Have you had enough?"

Julie thought he meant he hoped she had but she needed to know. She felt his honesty bringing them closer. "Tell me more, if you can bear to."

"After a while I came to my senses and took a hard line. It didn't work. That was when the marriage started to fall apart. I was faced with the choice of giving her all her own way, or splitting up. When I told her I was seriously considering divorcing her, she found a way she reckoned would bring me to heel. She began to see her old boyfriends, as if to say, 'I'll show you how many other men want me'."

"I'm sorry, Greg."

"More? You can stop me any time."

"It's not curiosity," Julie said earnestly, "I need to know. You've helped me so much. I want to do something in return. I don't like being in the dark. Can't you understand?"

He nodded and smiled, if faintly, but he seemed less reluctant as he began again.

"One day I had to go up to Rome from Amalfi on business. Sam said she planned to spend the day and the evening with friends, so there was no reason to hurry home. I called up a fellow I'd been doing business with whom I didn't know very well but who was a friend of hers. At first he didn't want to see me, which made me suspicious. Samantha had gone to Rome several times when we were on the yacht and, when I came to think about it, the last time Alessandro, that was his name, was in London when we were there, too, she had made excuses to go out without me.

"So I decided to see him. He was feeling pretty put out and ready to spill the beans. He told me Samantha had informed him that she was leaving me – and him, of course – justifying it by saying I had threatened to leave her first, and that she was going to join an Englishman she had once been going to marry and who had gone to Brazil. This chap told me she was getting a plane from Rome that evening for Paris, then flying to South America from there."

"Did you believe him?"

"Yes, I did. He was quite obviously telling the truth. I drove fast to the airport and tried to find out if Samantha had been on the last plane for Paris or if she was booked on a future one. I drew a blank there, so drove on down to the yacht. She was gone, all right, but her clothes were still there."

Julie had a memory flash of going to the wrong cabin that day in Amalfi; of seeing the racks of beautiful dresses behind the wardrobe doors . . .

"Go on," she said. He seemed to be miles away, as though he was remembering, too. She touched his hand softly. "Go on, Greg."

"I called up her friends," he continued. "They said she had lunch with them and they confirmed the fact that she was flying to Paris that night. But she hadn't caught a plane. Not using her own name, anyway. I telephoned her parents in London. They hadn't heard from her. They promised to contact me when they heard, but they never did.

"After a while, some weeks later, they grew alarmed because they were certain Samantha would have contacted them, wherever she was. They went to Rome and set up enquiries. Behind my back, I'm bound to say, which was a pity because we had been on good terms. But—" his eyes were hard, now.

"How did they get aboard?"

"They went to the man who looks after *Neptuna* when I'm away. He knew them and wasn't to know they didn't have permission. People do strange things when they're upset," said Greg, eyes lidded, looking down at his hands. "They

123

knew we weren't getting on well. And they knew Sam could drive people mad."

Wasn't that what Moira had said?

Greg continued, "Anyway, they found Sam's clothes on board and drew the wrong conclusions." He looked down at his hands again. "They decided I had done her in and went to the police. It's on the cards that I'll be charged with her murder." He cleared his throat and looked up at Julie, his eyes bleak. "Now you've had the story, shall we start enjoying ourselves? Here's the waiter. Chocolate gateaux?"

She wanted to say, 'It doesn't make any difference,' but that would be dishonest. In the telling, Greg's troubles, which had been a little unreal to her by comparison with her own, had taken on a validity that frightened her. She thought of her father in intensive care, the fear in her mother's face when Greg was mentioned. Her mother had read the papers and listened to gossip, as she had not. She probably already knew Greg could be charged with murder.

"Chocolate gateaux?" Greg said again. From the way he said it this time Julie knew that he was sorry he had given in to her and told her the truth. That perhaps with hindsight, in spite of her protest to the contrary, he had decided her wish to know was idle curiosity. She felt he had gone away somewhere in his mind and closed a gate behind him. "I'm sorry," she said, "to have put you through that."

"I understand that you would want to know. It makes a difference, though, doesn't it?"

They both became aware that a waiter was hovering, holding out the menu. They shook their heads.

"Café?"

"I don't think so," said Julie. She felt the evening had come to an end. Greg asked for the bill. She reached for her wrap. "I'm sorry," she said again.

"You will understand why I was reluctant to tell you. It's not as though you're an old friend," said Greg, "like Moira."

The words went through her heart like a knife.

She said in a soft, quick voice, "I love you, Greg. You've

come into my life when I need you, but I haven't anything to give to you. That's the truth of it. Don't say it's not much of a love. I have loved you ever since that first night you walked into the Villa Rosa and frightened the wits out of me. But you've come to me at the wrong time. I can't take this lot on top of . . . It's as though we're not meant to . . ."

It's as though we're being tested, she thought. "If Moira had telegraphed that first day that you were her friend and she hoped we'd have fun, I wouldn't have run away. I ran because I had a responsibility to her that I was obliged to put before you. Now there's this . . ." There were tears in her eyes. "I can't trust my mother not to worry my father with the fact that I'm involved with a man suspected of murder. My mother is my responsibility. She's hare-brained. And she stands between my father and me. I wish things could have been different." She looked up at him with love in her eyes and fear in her heart.

Greg said bleakly, "I do understand you've got enough on your plate, Julie. Come on, let's go."

Chapter Eight

Delia was waiting for her, her eyes accusing. "Where have you been?"

"I've been out to dinner," Julie snapped and was appalled at her tone. She was about to apologise when her mother said accusingly,

"So you were hungry, after all."

"I was not hungry when you ate yours. I don't want you to think I planned to go out after you left. I had a late invitation."

Clearly, Delia did not believe her. "May I ask if you've been out with that Strathallan man?"

"I have."

"Don't you read the papers, Julie?" Delia's voice was shrill. "Honestly, I despair of you."

"I shall in future read the papers," Julie spoke as evenly as her disturbed feelings would allow. "Mother, I'm upset. I would like to go to bed. I don't want to discuss Greg Strathallan. I recognise that my loyalty is here, with you and Father. I think Greg knows I can't complicate my life any further at the moment."

"You're not going to see him again?" Delia's eyes that a moment before were welling with tears became wary with ill-considered hope.

"I doubt very much if he would want to see me. We seem to have come to a natural parting of the ways. Mother, I want to go to bed. I have a lot of decisions to make tomorrow."

"What decisions?"

Julie smiled tiredly. She had been so full of life this evening until things went wrong. "I'm in charge here, now. I'm going to ring Anatole first thing tomorrow and see if his wife is well enough for him to come back at least part-time. I need a manager. I can't do what I have to do and run the hotel."

"What's the matter with Pierre? He seems to me to be a very good deputy. I don't know what you mean when you say 'what I have to do'," Delia said querulously.

Julie supposed it was natural that her mother, ignorant of the way the wheels ran in the running of hotels, should worry about Julie's lack of experience in view of her inability to guide her. "There's nothing wrong with Pierre," she said, "but Anatole has more clout with the staff. They haven't the same respect for Pierre."

Delia asked suspiciously, "What is it you have to do?"

"I have to do everything that Father normally does, you know that. I'm responsible for the overall working of the hotel. I have to make decisions."

"Can't decisions wait until your father is better?"

"Some can. But there'll be plenty that can't. The trouble is, Mother, I've come to realise that there are matters that concern me that I haven't been told about." She gave her mother a chance to reply.

Delia's lips tightened.

"If you don't tell me, then I'm going to have to pay a call on Oliver Wingate. Mother," said Julie in exasperation. "What's bugging me is there's something I'm quite sure you know about and you're not telling me. OK, this was valid when Father was in charge but it isn't now. I can't take over the responsibilities of management if I don't know what's going on."

Delia's face crumpled. "I can't give away your father's private affairs, dear. He would never forgive me."

"I don't think they're private affairs," Julie retorted. "I think they're my affairs as well as yours. Affairs that affect all of us. If you can't bear to take the responsibility for telling me yourself, for goodness' sake get his permission."

"You know they have expressly forbidden me to talk business to Neil," her mother wailed. "You know that."

Julie heaved a huge sigh. "All right, I'll have to be blunt. Does Father owe Oliver Wingate money?"

127

Delia gasped.

So Greg was right. "Why?" Julie asked. "Why would he have to borrow money?"

"I didn't say he did. And he didn't have to." Delia looked terribly upset. "I don't know anything about it. They had discussions. Neil agreed to . . . I don't know, Julie," she said distractedly. "I can't talk to you about business matters. I haven't been involved."

"Just confirm this," Julie said, coaxing her. "Oliver loaned us money?"

"You're not supposed to be involved, Julie."

"OK, I am involved. Tell me what you mean when you say Father didn't have to borrow the money."

"It wasn't his idea. Oliver thought the hotels needed brightening up. He was most insistent. And he was prepared to pay."

"So the money wasn't borrowed?"

"Not in that sense. He called it an investment."

So that was it! Oliver Wingate had infiltrated the Creighton business! What had Greg said about the partnership? That Oliver Wingate eats her father's type for breakfast. Julie felt chilled. "So if we don't go through with the amalgamation we're in debt to Martin's father over something he forced on Father? Shoved money in his pocket, did he? Forced Father to make improvements so that, in his opinion, the hotels would be more valuable?"

"Julie, I don't know you when you talk like this. You've become hard." Delia looked distraught.

"I've become businesslike. It wasn't necessary before, when Father carried the can. I could afford to be the pampered daughter. But I'm the boss now. And you're making life impossible for me by keeping me in the dark. Now, tell me how much money is involved."

Delia looked scared.

"I have to know, Mother. It looks as though this amalgamation isn't going through. Not if it depends on my marrying Martin. And that is the crux of the matter, isn't it? That's where things have gone wrong. Instead of Father saying, 'We'll have the amalgamation if Julie and Martin marry', he has said this: 'The amalgamation is a fact and to make it work, because I don't trust Oliver Wingate, Julie has to marry Martin. That way she can keep an eye on the family interests'."

Delia began to cry.

Julie hardened her heart. "So, I'm asking you again, how much money has changed hands?"

Delia wiped her eyes. "Neil doesn't tell me those things."

It wasn't a straight answer, but Julie felt she was probably telling the truth. Anyway, she felt she couldn't press her any further. "I'm calling a staff meeting for ten o'clock," she said. "You're welcome to attend."

"Of course I'd like to, dear," her mother replied, "but your father wouldn't be happy if I turned up late at the hospital saying I'd been to a business meeting. You know how he prefers not to bother me with these things."

Thank God for that, Julie thought. She had not anticipated for one moment that her mother would attend the staff meeting. But at least, she thought, having been invited, if matters become more acrimonious between us, she won't be able to say I'm making decisions behind her back.

She did not sleep well. Her own troubles fused with Greg's until she saw them as one. Moira was right, she said to herself, I cannot absorb all this and deal with it. A sick father. An incompetent mother. A fiancé with a mistress. She thought of the sapphire ring that was back in her possession and what it signified. She thought of the warmth Greg had shown her. The solidarity. The fun. Again his solidarity. He was as solid as the black rocks of the Italian coastline.

She did not, could not believe that he would have harmed this difficult wife of his. She remembered how angry he had been that time she put herself in danger by diving in when the yacht's engines were going. Yes, he was tough. But not a murderer. She remembered how he had covered her up with a sheet so that she would not get sunburned as she lay on the deck of his motor yacht. The expensive toy he had bought for Samantha. She worried about the fact that he had not wanted to talk about his problems. About the fact that she had forced the story out of him. About the fact that she had sincerely wanted to help until she understood, until he told her, the extent of his trouble.

They were both on their own, now.

She wakened heavy-eyed. In the mirror she saw the lines of strain. She showered and dressed in a favourite suit that was at least three years old. A dressmaker had shortened it to a fashionable length. This was not a day to wear anything that had been made new for her marriage. She picked up her handbag. It slipped out of her hands. She went down on her knees to pick up the contents that had fallen on to the floor. Powder compact. Comb. Then she saw the sapphire ring Martin had insisted on slipping back on her finger. She put it in her pocket.

As she was about to leave the room she caught a glimpse of herself in the full length wardrobe mirror. Long legs. Long fair hair. She felt a lump in her throat. Felt tears begin to prick behind her eyes. She realised then that she no longer believed it was her looks that had attracted Greg. She tried to put her personal problems out of her mind. She telephoned Anatole, the manager who was on leave.

"Anatole, how is Bettine?"

"Not well enough to leave, Julie." He sounded despondent.

"I presume you would like to come back to work."

"Of course."

"I've got a proposition to put to you. Would you bring her in here if a room could be found for her? That way you could get on with your work and also keep an eye on her. Her meals could be sent up from the kitchens."

Anatole was delighted. "One moment. I must ask her."

"Of course. Tell her I would send a car."

It didn't take any time at all to persuade Bettine. "She thinks that is a good idea. When can we come, Julie?" He was overjoyed. "I wish I had thought of it before."

"It wasn't so necessary before, Anatole. Thank you very much. And thank Bettine. I'll see about the car and the room. Then someone will ring and tell you what arrangements we have made."

"Thank you, Julie. Thank you. *Merci.* How very pleased I am."

She went back to the dressing table feeling good. So, that was easy. Now for the next move. She took a hairbrush, swathed her hair round her head then pinned it in place. As if I can make a different kind of person of myself, she thought. Maybe I can become a woman who is able to shoulder everybody's problems. I, who am not experienced at dealing with trouble at its source. I have had a feather-bed existence. Everyone has been nice to me because I am my father's daughter. Now I am on my own and in one move I have dealt with Anatole's troubles as well as a section of my own.

She asked the office to book her a flight to Heathrow. Then she called the housekeeper and asked her to prepare a room for Bettine.

"*Deuxième étage. Seize,* M'selle," she responded promptly.

"That one is free? Right, I'd be pleased if you would get it prepared."

She spoke to her secretary about making arrangements for Bettine to be picked up. The staff assembled in her office dead on time. Standing facing them, looking at their faces, she was shaken to see the level of anxiety there. She spoke about her father first. Told them he was holding his own. "Whatever your problems are, you must come to me." She paused. "I know you're worried about the amalgamation."

Pierre spoke up. "There are those of us who wouldn't work for Mr Wingate," he said. "Sorry to have to say it, M'selle but someone has to. I think you ought to know some of the staff will be leaving."

Oh no! She hadn't expected mutiny. "Would those of you who would leave like to tell me why?"

A murmur went round the room. They exchanged glances. One of the waiters said diffidently, "He hires and fires a lot."

Then the English Harry spoke up. It was clear he was choosing his words carefully. "Mr Wingate's methods are quite different from your father's. He would change the character of the hotel. He doesn't believe in family hotels."

Julie felt chilled. "But why would he want to amalgamate with family hotels if he didn't believe in them?"

She waited. Uncomfortable glances were exchanged. Then it was Harry who spoke again. "I've worked for him," he said. "Before he got the Silvine. You'll know he had a number of smaller hotels at different times. He smartened them up and sold them. We wouldn't like your hotels to be smartened up, Julie. Or sold. Would you?"

Julie said, "My father wouldn't allow it. It's only an amalgamation. It's not a take-over."

She was aware that eyes slid away as she tried to meet them.

Pierre said, "He's a tough boss. We understand you wouldn't know him as a businessman. You'd only have seen his social side."

"Yes." She had to admit that. But her father must have looked beyond his social side.

Georges the Commissionaire spoke up. "All three of your hotels are a byword for dignity," he said. "That's what your clièntele like. *Dignité*. Mr Wingate does not think much of *dignité*."

Harry spoke up. "Americans call his system 'making a fast buck.' We don't wish to criticise him, Julie, please understand. But we want you to know it would be very different if your father couldn't come back to work and he were to take charge."

Julie wanted to say that she would be in charge. She wished she could say it, with confidence. She thought about the fact that she had not been consulted with regard to the amalgamation. She had to face the fact that she had been an employee, privileged, certainly, but not so very different from these people lined up before her. She was often asked for ideas, yes, but she could not honestly say she was seriously consulted.

"I'm sure you know I'm not allowed to talk to my father about business," she said. "In fact, I'm not even welcome to visit him because the hospital staff see me as representing business. So what I intend to do is without his blessing. I want you to understand that. And I hope you will rally behind me. Anatole is coming back." She told them about the plan to move Bettine in. "He will be able to take over and keep an eye on her at the same time. They will be in room sixteen on the second floor."

There was a murmur of assent. *"Bon."*

"I am going to London today, and I'm going to see Mr Wingate. You will know I haven't the authority to cancel the amalgamation."

"No, of course." *Vraiment.*

"But at least it shouldn't be too difficult to block any further interference until my father is better."

A sigh whispered round the room. Julie hoped their relief would prove to be justified. She was frightened, now she saw the impact the proposed amalgamation had had on the staff. Why had they not told her father? She could only think they had felt reasonably safe while he was in charge, and with the knowledge that Julie was marrying into the enemy camp.

"You all know I've had no experience of being totally in charge." Wasn't that what they were saying? "If I make mistakes I shall expect you to tell me."

They crowded round her to shake her hand in the French way. "You've taken a great load off our minds."

"We understand."

"You can count on us."

She was warmed by their goodwill. As they filed out she turned to Pierre. "You got my flight booked?"

"Of course. Twelve o'clock, as you wanted."

"Thank you. I'm off now. Will you send someone up for my bag and ask Georges to get me a taxi, please."

"À bientot."

She sat back in the taxi watching the rushing traffic, biting her lips with nervousness. Everything had happened too suddenly. She was not prepared for her confrontation with Martin's father. She had never had any reason to stand up to him. As her potential father-in-law he had been avuncular with her. Now she was coming in as an enemy. She was going to have to ask him some very awkward questions.

How does a girl in her early twenties ask a man of fifty if it is true that he has threatened to break her father? And

133

how? And for what reason? She took out the leather-backed, loose-leafed notebook she always carried with her. She chewed the end of her pen. In the end she put it away again. She was going to have to play this interview by ear.

Arriving at Heathrow she looked at the long queue waiting for taxis then turned back impatiently and took the Underground. As she went down the stairs and stepped aboard the train she thought of Greg who owned a yacht and travelled sometimes by bus. She shook the thought away as irrelevant, knowing it was not.

A taxi took her directly to the Hotel Silvine, the big glass-fronted tower in Hyde Park. She went through the door carrying her small overnight bag and approached the desk. A pretty red-haired girl was handing a key to a guest. Julie had not seen her before. But then, she did not by any means know all the staff, though they no doubt knew her for they would be interested in the girl the Wingate son was going to marry. They would have seen her photo in the papers. It registered on her mind that this girl was looking at her oddly.

"I want to see Mr Wingate, please," she said, holding the nervousness at bay.

"He's not here," the girl said. Her cheeks had reddened. "You mean Martin?"

"No. I want to see his father." She wondered why the girl looked so disconcerted.

"I'm sorry. I assumed . . . I mean . . ."

"What's the matter?" asked Julie.

"It's just that – he's in a meeting."

But it wasn't just that, Julie could see. Her eyes narrowed. "Has he said he doesn't want to see me? You obviously know who I am."

"He really is in a meeting. If you could wait . . ." The girl broke off and said in a low, breathless voice, "I'm Antonia."

Antonia! Martin's mistress. Back in England as was Martin! So he had set up two homes for her! One in Paris. The other at his parents' hotel? Presumably where he could live with her? Julie overcame her shock and disbelief.

Wasn't this, after all, a good thing? Even recognising that, she had difficulty suppressing her anger and very real humiliation.

Antonia found her voice first. "Perhaps we should have a talk."

"Yes, I think I would like that. But you're working."

Antonia said, "I could get someone to take over from me. I would be about five minutes. Would you like to go to the first floor, to the Peacock Lounge, and wait for me there?"

Julie nodded. "All right."

Ignoring the lift, she walked up the stairs in a daze.

The lounge was a glimmering blue, furnished with glass tables and ultra-modern chairs with strange backs and hard seats. There were murals on the walls, peacocks strutting. Potted plants merged colourfully with the jungle pictures behind them. There was nobody else in the room. Julie sat down in one of the window seats, looking out over Hyde Park.

Presently Antonia came. She sat opposite and Julie had an opportunity to study her face for the first time. She had quaint features, short nose, wide-set eyes, and a very determined chin. There was a steely strength about her that Julie did not possess.

Julie asked tentatively, "How did you come to be working here?" She felt no resentment now. Only shock remained.

"Martin asked me to." Now it was the other girl's turn to look at Julie. "There's no point in you and I being enemies," she said. "I asked you up here because I think it's high time you learned the truth. I tried to warn you by writing to your mother when you became engaged to Martin but you didn't take any notice."

Julie wished the stunned feeling would go away.

"This isn't a very nice story," said Antonia, "and I'm not proud of my part in it, but it's the truth. Martin wants to marry you and hang on to me. If you go ahead with the marriage it will be half a life for both of us. Don't imagine he's going to give me up," she said with awesome candour. "He isn't."

It was ludicrous, but it was happening. Julie's mind was

135

spinning round in circles. She said, "I don't understand why you didn't opt out. Go away. If he's not going to marry you—"

The other girl leaned forward, looking earnestly into Julie's face. "Neither is he going to let me go," she said.

"You want him to? To let you go?"

"No . . ."

"Then why not?" Julie asked incredulously. "If he's never going to marry you, why not disappear?"

The girl's face was all at once a picture of misery. "I could not disappear," she said. "Martin would find me."

"Oh come on! He's not Sherlock Holmes."

"You don't understand," Antonia said. "I would want to be found. Martin and I are in love and no material arrangements could ever stand in the way." She added unkindly, with a touch of scorn, "You probably don't understand. You've probably never been in love – like this."

Julie looked back at her with stony eyes, thinking of Greg.

Antonia said, "None of this is your fault except that you might have talked to me after I wrote that letter to your mother."

"Perhaps I would have," Julie retorted, stung to a sharp reply, "if you had written it to me. My parents want me to marry Martin, so I wasn't shown the letter." Antonia's eyes widened.

"He's only marrying you for your father's hotels," she said. "You ought to know that. I shall go on fighting, even if you do marry him. And if I win—" Antonia looked at Julie with bright, hard eyes – "If I get him back after your marriage, you stand to lose a great deal."

"What do you mean?" Even as she asked Julie knew the answer. Answers, even. Antonia sharing her husband. And that was only the beginning. Greg had said Oliver Wingate was ruthless. Ruthless enough to plot for Martin to get the Creighton hotels, or part of them, in a divorce settlement?

Antonia gave her the answer. "You know about property

136

in divorces. And lawyers can fight dirty. The Wingate lawyers can. Anyway, I'm not saying that is in Martin's plans. He may want to stay married to you, but I would be there. Always," said Antonia defiantly and with conviction.

The shock had gone. Julie felt numb. "Knowing all this, you can still love him?" she asked in disbelief.

Antonia nodded. "We were born for each other. Everyone has faults." She was yet again defiant. "You have to be forgiving, sometimes."

Julie looked at her with sorrow and in her heart wished her well. "Where is Martin?"

"At his country house."

"What?"

Antonia's piquant face showed amazement. "You must surely know about Martin's antique business?"

"He told me he had given up all that."

Antonia laughed softly.

Julie added, her cheeks going pink, "He told his father that, too. He intends to work in the hotels."

"Then I will tell you something that might interest you. Martin has bought a big Queen Anne house in Berkshire and he's busy filling it with antiques. If you marry him that's where you'll live, don't have any doubt about it. You won't have any part in the running of your family business. Martin hates hotels. He has always wanted to work among antiques, and now he has achieved it you're never going to get him away. As his father knows very well."

"His father told my father—"

The other girl silenced her.

"Stop believing these people, Julie. They're not telling the truth."

Julie started to say with awe, "This is the family you want to marry in—"

Antonia broke in with a kind of weary complaisance. "I've always known Martin is a liar. I'm resigned to it."

There seemed nothing more to say. "Have you got the address of this house?"

Antonia gave it to her. Julie took her notebook from her briefcase and wrote it down. "It's easy to find," Antonia said. "I think you'll find Martin there now." She added in a small voice, "Since he wasn't with you."

"What do you mean?" Julie's eyes flew open.

"He didn't come back last night. I thought he was with you."

Again, Julie felt that unwilling sense of pity.

"And don't think he's double crossing his father," Antonia added. "Oliver knows the truth. He's only about fifty. He's prepared to run all the hotels. Wants to. Now your father is ill—" She broke off and with a change of tone said, "I'm sorry about your father. Believe me when I say Oliver isn't. He thinks his ship has come home."

Julie tucked the notebook back in her briefcase and rose. "I think he may find his ship has foundered," she said grimly. "Thank you for talking to me."

Antonia also rose. "Are you going to let him go?" she asked, and now she looked wan and rather sad.

"You're welcome to him," Julie retorted. "I only hope he marries you, and that you're happy."

"I haven't anything to give him."

Julie wondered with very real compassion if that was her answer.

Her father's Rover was kept in the Merrion's basement garage. Julie went straight to the hotel, left her bag, consulted a road map, took the car keys from the office and set out for Berkshire. Rain had begun to fall, a soft, cool autumn rain, scarcely enough to help the gardens out of their summer dryness. The traffic was not heavy. She drove fast. The village was only a couple of miles off the main road. She found the house easily enough. It was right on the edge of a pretty village built around a cricket green. There were several period houses adjacent advertising cream teas. An ideal situation, she thought sardonically, for an antique shop. Easily discovered by Sunday drivers and cricket fans.

Martin's premises were in a beautiful building, old brick with white-painted windows and a slate roof. She parked outside and hurried up the path to ring the bell. She rang it again and again but there was no reply. Eventually she came back down the steps and peered through a low front window.

There was a big room, furnished with a large gilt mirror over the fireplace, an eighteenth-century bookcase standing empty against the wall, a Turkish carpet. In the corner there was what looked like a seventeenth-century desk. Turning up the collar of her coat against the rain, Julie crossed the path and looked in the window on the opposite side. Here also was a beautifully proportioned room but the furniture had not yet been arranged. There was a round table inlaid with brass, some pretty Regency chairs, a rolled-up carpet leaning against the wall, a magnificent sideboard.

Following the path, she made her way round the house looking in windows. Each room was the same. His father knows, Antonia had said. Indeed he did. Martin could never have financed this on his own.

Julie stood at the back door, her eyes bright with anger as she looked round. A hundred yards away lay a stable block. As she stood there, a man crossed the yard and unlocked a massive door. She hurried over. The stable was stacked floor to ceiling with furniture. As she stepped off the grass on to stone paving, the man heard her and turned.

"I'm looking for Martin Wingate," she said.

"He'll be back in a few moments," the man replied. "Have you got an appointment with him?"

"No, I came to talk to him. About antiques," she added.

"We're not really open for business yet," the man told her. "But if there's something you're particularly keen to have, I dare say Mr Wingate may oblige you. Would you like to wait for him?" Julie nodded. "If you'll hold on a moment I'll let you in."

"Thank you." Julie hurried back across the grass. "Does he live here?" she asked.

"He's moving in just as soon as he's got all the stuff sorted out," the man replied. "He's getting married soon." He smiled at Julie. "There you are, my dear," he said as he opened the door. There was the sound of a car and both of them turned. "Ah, there he is now," said the man. "I'll be off back to my work, then."

139

Julie stood in the doorway as Martin came up the path. Martin, whom she had loved and trusted and wanted to marry. Martin with his easy charm, his tawny brown eyes and his lively, boyish air. His enthusiasms – and his lies. He saw her and, unbelievably, held both arms wide. But then, she thought, wasn't he accustomed to Antonia forgiving him?

"So it's true," she said as he came closer.

Martin's arms dropped to his sides.

She said bleakly, "Your man told me you're getting married. May I ask who the lucky girl is? Your receptionist at the Silvine? Or me?"

Martin's arms were once more outstretched to embrace her. She backed away. "You've been lying all along, Martin. You never intended to live at the Merrion and run it with me. You've been stringing my family along so that your family can get an interest in our hotels."

"Julie! Let's talk," he beseeched her, his tawny eyes winningly soft.

"There's been enough talk," she replied curtly. "And I've seen all I need to see. I'm going straight to your father." As she spoke she remembered what Greg had said, 'Bear in mind what I've told you when you go to see Martin and you may find yourself cured, and free.' "You're not going to marry me, Martin Wingate, now or at any time. I suggest you marry that poor foolish girl who is working at Reception in the Silvine."

"Julie." He grasped her arm, but she swung away, ran across the hall. She flung the door open. Slamming it behind her she sped to her car, jumped in and started the engine. What to do now? Go and see Oliver Wingate? Or return to Paris and talk to her father? There was really no choice. She headed for London and the Silvine.

Antonia, to her great relief, had gone off duty. Julie asked to see Oliver Wingate and was shown up to his office, a chrome-and-plate-glass room on the fourth floor overlooking the park. There was an executive desk topped with red leather, an enormous leather chair, a cocktail cabinet. Wingate was totally unlike his son. He was stocky, sandy-haired and already going bald.

"Why, Julie," he exclaimed with what seemed like genuine pleasure. "How nice to see you. I thought you were in Paris."

"I was. I came over to see Martin."

"How nice. Do sit down, my dear."

"Thank you. I'd rather stand. I have seen Martin," she said, her eyes steadily on his face. "I've been to his house in Berkshire and discovered that he has gone back on his word about the antiques business. I've also discovered that you are employing his girlfriend Antonia here in Reception. I get the impression they're living together."

Momentarily, Wingate's face closed. Then he seemed to contain the initial shock. "Come, Julie. Sit down. Let's have a drink together and talk this over." He headed across the room to the cocktail cabinet.

"What has to be said can be said quite briefly," Julie told him. "I really don't want a drink. You know how ill my father is. He can't deal with this matter, so it's between you and me."

"Let's start at the beginning, shall we?" suggested Wingate suavely. "When a man is jilted virtually at the altar steps, there's no accounting for what he will do."

"I had a very good reason for not marrying him," she retorted. "What I'm telling you I discovered today already existed at that time. Martin has an enormous stock of furniture in that house in Berkshire. It was very clear to me that he has owned the house for a considerable time. It's not possible for him to have found it, for the sale to have gone through, and for him to stock it as he has done in the time since we were supposed to have married." She waited to give Wingate a chance to reply but he merely gazed at her, his eyes cold, his colour heightened beneath the sandy hair. "Martin didn't have the money to set that up," she went on. "It represents an enormous investment."

She waited for him to admit his interest.

He said, "Martin has a winning way with him. I dare say he got round his bank manager."

"It doesn't matter where the money came from," retorted Julie, certain he was lying. "You knew about the venture. That's what I am saying to you. *You knew*. Anyway, although my father hasn't confided in me exactly how committed he and you are to this amalgamation, I want to get out."

"Out? Oh no."

He spoke with such confidence that Julie felt a stab of fear.

She tried desperately not to show it. "You set the amalgamation up on a false premise," she said. "I don't know if you knew at the time that Martin was not going to work for you."

"I didn't," Wingate admitted. He seemed to be telling the truth.

"But you do know now?"

He said unhappily, "It's become increasingly obvious." The drink forgotten, he sat down behind his desk and began doodling on a pad. The fight seemed suddenly to have gone out of him. "I'm no more happy about what Martin is doing than you are, Julie. I had to help him – or lose him. He is our only son. Don't you see?"

Julie felt her anger slipping. "I'm sorry."

"Yes, well . . ." Wingate doodled some more on the pad. He looked tired and, she thought, rather sad. "I'm sorry about all this. Let's get Martin down and talk to him, work something out."

"No. It's too late for that. I couldn't marry the kind of man I now discover Martin to be." She stood across the desk and looked down at him, feeling a certain compassion. "You'll let my father off the hook?"

"No," he said abruptly and quite, quite definitely. "No, I can't do that. That's quite another matter. That's business."

Julie realised then how ill-equipped she was to deal with this kind of man. She was very frightened. She thought of her father, too ill to be told what was going on. Of her mother, so helpless and unbusinesslike. Greg, who had said Oliver Wingate ate people like them for breakfast. She had

142

to manage. She said, "My father made these arrangements believing Martin, his son-in-law to be, would be working in the business. Since Martin never intended to, I think it could be said he's not obliged to go on."

Wingate said smoothly, "You're making assumptions. I'm sure he hasn't said that to you."

She didn't answer.

"Has he?" Wingate's eyes were hard, and at the same time, triumphant.

She couldn't answer because she would have to tell the truth, that he hadn't. I'm getting into deep water here, she thought. She had no authority to talk to Wingate like this.

He could see her uncertainty. She read it in his sharp eyes. "There's something you may not realise," he said smoothly. "Did you know your father owes me a tidy sum?"

But she did. "It will be repaid," she said.

"Fifty thousand pounds."

She managed to speak coolly, as though it was a meagre sum, "I'm sure something can be arranged about repayment." Icily polite, she enquired, "May I ask how this came about?"

"There were refurbishings and new decorations for the Geneva hotel."

She remembered the letter from Le Bosquet's manager that she had found in her father's files and rounded on him furiously. "I was at Le Bosquet only six months ago. It did not need redecorating. You talked my father into this, didn't you?"

"We agreed," he replied.

"But you had the money, and you pressed it. My father would never have suggested it himself. He never once commented to me that there was any work to be done at Le Bosquet. It's the kind of thing the family discuss – always." Did they, still. She had to recognise that things had changed. Her father was no longer confiding in her.

Wingate gave the vaguest of shrugs. "Since we were amalgamating, it was in my interests to have Le Bosquet in tiptop condition."

"The money will be repaid," she said, feeling sick. She went out, closing the door quietly behind her.

She drove back to the Merrion and put the car away. What to do now? She remembered that Greg had offered to help her with money. But that was before the strained silence. Before recognition of her responsibilities and the overwhelming nature of her problems. Before fear took over and an inner knowledge crept in that together they could not win. She went up to the family's apartment, sat down in the telephone chair and dialled Directory Enquiries. I am becoming accustomed to eating humble pie, she said to herself. I have pronounced myself a businesswoman. Businesswomen cannot afford pride. Not when their father's life is at stake. There will be plenty of humble pie to eat if I have to marry Martin in order to extricate the family from this mess. I may as well get in some practice. Then she remembered Oliver Wingate saying with reference to the fifty thousand pounds, "That's business," separating it from friendship and love. Why should she not ask Greg to help on that level? She jotted down the number given her by the disembodied voice, and dialled.

"Strathallan, Butler and Headingly," said a girl at the other end of the line.

"I'd like to talk to Mr Strathallan please."

"Who is speaking?"

"A friend. It's personal."

"I'm sorry," said the voice. "He went to Geneva on business. I'm not sure when he will be back in London."

"Geneva?" And then, before she could stop herself, she had blurted out, "I saw him in Paris yesterday."

"He telephoned to say he was going on to Geneva."

"When do you expect him to return?"

"He didn't say. If you give me your name—"

"Thank you," said Julie quickly. "I'll ring again."

She asked the office to see if they could get her on a flight to Paris. Why had Greg not mentioned he was going to Geneva today? He must surely have known last night. Maybe not. Hadn't she brought an overnight bag with her this morning, not knowing she would be going home

144

again today? People did things suddenly all the time. Some unexpected business could have come up. But why Geneva? Le Bosquet was in Geneva. What had that to do with Greg's going there? Nothing, of course. How could it?

She took the keys of the penthouse that was being done up for herself and Martin and went in the lift to the top floor. She and Martin had planned the alterations. They had consulted the architect together. And all the time he had known they were never going to live there! She couldn't believe it. Yes, she could, in view of what she now knew about Martin.

She unlocked the outer door. Went in. A considerable amount of work had been done. Walls had been plastered. Several window enlarged. The bathroom harboured a box of tiles and the handbasin she had chosen was lying on the floor. Who was paying for this work, she wondered now. She had understood the apartment to be a present from her parents. It had to be. "Our wedding gift to you." She remembered Delia saying the words.

She made a note to ring the builder and ask him to put the conversion on hold.

She went back to the family apartment and was about to make herself a cup of tea when the desk rang to say they had got her a flight back to Paris. "I'll get you a taxi. You've just got time, Julie, but you'd better hurry."

"Coming." She picked up her bag, glad to have to shelve her problems, at least for the time being.

But they toppled off their shelf as she sat in the back of the taxi looking blindly out at the buildings rushing by, and the traffic. She remembered Antonia saying the Wingate lawyers fought dirty. She was certain her father would not engage lawyers who fought dirty in return. But anyway, Oliver Wingate's thrusting money into her father's hands and been wily, but it could scarcely be said to be criminal. Neil, she conceded, had been a fool. At best, pliant. The cold truth, as she saw it, was that her father had accepted fifty thousand pounds from Wingate and she had to find a way to pay it back without incurring further expense. She put her hand in her pocket, reaching for a tissue, and her fingers touched Martin's ring. Its presence there seemed like a dreadful omen.

They were at Heathrow. The car moved in to the pavement and came to a halt. She paid the driver and picking up her things made her way towards her flight desk. The laughter and chatter of the hurrying crowds shed loneliness over her. She remembered taking this trip with Greg when he was on his way to Amalfi to an interview with the police. He had not told her what happened. She had not asked him. Would he take her silence for indifference?

Sitting in the plane looking down as the blue-grey waters of the Channel passed beneath them she thought about the coming interview with her mother. Wished she hadn't told her she was going to London. In the event that she had returned on the same day it had proved unnecessary. She would expect to be told what had happened. She would panic.

Why had Greg not said he was going to Geneva today? Because he had gone on business. Why should she consider his movements were any concern of hers? She had a window seat and the evening sun slanted in as they left the Channel behind. The stewardess offered her a drink. She thanked her, contemplating with dread this evening's interview with her mother.

The plane came in to a smooth landing. She gathered up her things. She thought, I cannot face my mother. Not yet. I will go and see Moira. She had the excuse of the wedding dress. Was it too late? She looked at her watch. Moira often stayed late at the salon. She found a telephone booth.

"Lovely to hear from you, *cherie*," Moira trilled.

"So you're still there. Do you never go home?"

"This is part of my home. Nobody comes to my apartment. Everyone comes here, you know that. You are coming to see me?"

"If you're free. Are you alone?"

"There is a friend with me but she is off very shortly to get a plane to Geneva. Such jet set friends I have!" Moira exclaimed.

Geneva! And Moira had said 'she'. As Julie went to look

for a taxi she asked hersef why she should automatically connect this woman with Greg. She knew why. Because Moira and Greg had many friends in common. She sat back in the taxi feeling upset.

As the taxi drew in to the curb in front of Moira's salon the door opened and a tall, well-dressed woman, classically beautiful with blonde hair swept back from her face, strode long-leggedly out and turned towards the Arc de Triomphe, hurrying. Then she saw a white Citroën parked a hundred yards away. The woman opened the door on the passenger side and slipped in. The car sped away. Julie remained glued to her seat. She wanted to cry.

The taxi driver looked round impatiently. *"C'est l'addresse correct?"*

She apologised, climbed out and paid him.

Moira was effusive in her welcome. "Such fun I am having, with all my friends dropping in. But I never get any work done."

"Greg's friends, too." Julie hadn't meant to say that. The words slipped out.

Moira hesitated only a second, then replied lightly, "Of course. Come and sit down. Put your bag in the corner."

Julie did as she asked and followed her up the steps to the little room at the back of the salon. "Isn't life full of coincidences?" she said. "My taxi just happened to pull in as your friend who is going to Geneva slipped into Greg's car. And he's going to Geneva, too. Is it possible you got rid of her when I rang?"

"If I did, I didn't succeed very well," Moira observed drily. "Let me pour you a drink, Julie. It will relax you. Look here," she continued, tapping her gently on the arm, "I told you before, Greg Strathallen is trouble. You have troubles of your own."

Julie recognised she had said this to Greg. But she had told him she loved him. She had talked about timing. She couldn't believe he would react by taking another woman on a jaunt to Switzerland.

"Do you think two lots of troubles put together cancel each other out?" Moira was asking. "I assure you, they do

147

not." She took two glasses from a cupboard and a bottle from the fridge.

"Who was the girl? At least you can tell me who she is."

"A friend from Italy. I have many Italian friends because I am Italian," said Moira expansively. "You know that. Here, drink this."

Julie took the glass. Moira glanced out of the window into the little courtyard. "My geraniums, are they not wonderful? They are so sheltered here they don't know the summer is fading. See, I have put in lights so that we can appreciate them at night."

"I wish you would be more straightforward with me," muttered Julie.

Moira made a sound like Phiiitt! "What you are saying is you wish all your troubles would go away. I cannot do that for you." She drew a chair close to where Julie sat and seated herself facing her. "Greg has been badly hurt. He fell in love once, very deeply, and he isn't going to do it again. Not so soon, anyway. You must believe it."

I do not believe it, Julie said to herself. He has fallen in love with me. I have said the timing was not right. But time passes.

Moira reached across the space between them and laid a comforting hand on Julie's arm. "I worry about you, *cherie*. You, too, have had a bad time. And I feel responsible for your meeting Greg. That's what I have to live with, sending you to the Villa Rosa at that most unfortunate time, not knowing Greg was there."

Julie sipped her wine. He loved me. And he has gone off with another woman. I cannot bear it.

"You have fallen in love with him," Moira went on. "That I can see. You can only get more hurt that way. Greg's a wonderful person but he has been through a great deal. Is still going through it. And heaven knows what will be the outcome."

"Tell me about Samantha."

"Greg has not told you?"

"Yes. But I want to hear about her from you."

148

"Sam was a strange sort of girl," Moira said. "She would court danger for danger's sake. I've seen her taunt Greg not far short of breaking point, time and again. This is why he is suspected of foul play. Sam's parents know him. They have seen the taunting, and his reactions. They talked about this to the police. They put ideas into heads. Everyone knows any man can be tried too far. You don't know Greg as I do. He can be tough."

She did know. She remembered again thoughtlessly diving into the bay when *Neptuna*'s engines were running, and his reaction. She had not considered it excessive in view of her stupidity. She thought he had been frightened for her, more than angry. But yes, she understood he could be tough. She blurted out, "You surely don't believe—"

Moira cut in. "I believe that in certain circumstances human beings can be provoked into anything. That's all I'm going to say. I'm a realist. If you're asking if Greg is guilty that is not my affair. I am concerned for him in this terrible business he has to go through. I am equally concerned for you. Even without the possibility of his being arrested, he has to get Samantha out of his system. He has to learn to trust again."

He had trusted her with the story of the dilemma and she had let him down. Tears came into Julie's eyes.

"Greg is also tough and strong," said Moira. "He can cope with his troubles."

Was rushing off to Switzerland with another woman his way of coping with them? Julie tried to understand.

In that quicksilver way that was a part of her charm Moira said, "Why don't you and I go to Positano for a few days? Forget a little."

Forget? No. She was not in a position to forget anything. "You're awfully kind, Moira. But my father is still in hospital. I've put myself in charge."

Moira brushed her words aside. "You've said you can't see him. You said you are a reminder of his problems. One thing at a time. Of course he must be left in peace to get better. I am sure your mother is managing very well. Leave her to persuade him you can't marry Martin."

Julie took another sip of her wine. "When I came here I was thinking about the wedding dress. We have to discuss that. Is there any chance that you might sell it?"

"You have to do nothing of the kind. We will deal with the dress some time. Not now. I have suggested we take two or three days off and go to the villa. I could get away the day after tomorrow. Whenever it suits you. In such places troubles are easily shelved."

Fifty thousand pounds worth of troubles was a lot to shelve, Julie thought grimly. She did not see a couple of days in the sun melting them away.

She felt tired and mixed-up in her mind.

"What are you thinking, *cherie*?"

"I feel empty. Lost. Totally without confidence." Julie's lower lip trembled. "I don't know what to do."

"I am telling you what to do. Come to Positano for a few days. In the sun we will concentrate on your problems. Or perhaps in the sun they will melt away. You have said yourself your mother spends all her time at the hospital. You cannot go with her. What are we waiting for?"

"You are very kind, Moira."

"It is nothing. A selfishness, surely. My guilty conscience is bothering me and I wish to get rid of it. If I had not sent you to the Villa Rosa alone you would not have met Greg."

"Does anything happen accidentally?"

"Fate I can cope with," retorted Moira briskly. "I quite simply do not believe in it. We are going together to Positano? Yes?"

Beautiful Positano, where she had fallen in love with Greg. Julie wished Moira was inviting her to some other place. "I don't know. I will have to think about it."

Chapter Nine

Julie made her way home feeling vaguely comforted, a little stronger and grateful for Moira's friendship. With her brief-case in one hand and her overnight bag in the other she walked down the Rue de la Grand Armée in the direction of the Arc de Triomphe, taking her time. When had she last eaten? At breakfast. She turned down a side street, veered left, then right. Ahead there was a restaurant she knew. Brightly clothed tables set out on the pavement.

She sat down. Settled her bags at her feet. Diners at adjacent tables glanced up briefly. A man who had been passing paused hopefully, smiling. She looked away. The waiter brought a menu. She ordered an omelette. Sitting there, she recognised that it was not just hunger that had brought her here, but reluctance to go home. She pondered on this unlikely alliance with her dressmaker.

Where were her old friends? She had scarcely noticed them drifting away. Martin's friends had not become hers. How could they, knowing about his attachment to Antonia, and Antonia's very real love for him?

She began to see how isolated she had become as a result of living 'over the shop' as her father described it. Living over the shop with her family had resulted in the very close ties that held them, and that was good. She ought not to blame her parents for seeing her as an integral part of the business. She must be partially to blame. She was twenty-three. She could have seen what was happening.

Time to take stock. She had been wrong to quarrel with her mother. She felt she had begun to see what Delia was doing. Muddling along on the few titbits of information about the business that Neil allowed her. Holding out on

Julie as her father had done because she was too young to be burdened with the really serious matters.

She thought about the fact that Delia deferred to Neil all the time. Neil was gentle but he was the boss and Delia not only understood that, she liked it. Was it then possible, Julie wondered, fiddling with her omelette, separating the bacon, forking it up with a piece of tomato, that if she wielded the upper hand, albeit velvet gloved, Delia might settle down and recognise, even with relief, that she was capable of holding the reins safely?

But she couldn't take up the reins without knowing the background to her problems. She must first persuade her mother to tell her how Neil had come to accept the money. For refurbishing, Wingate had said. She supposed that by comparison with the gaudy murals and modern furnishings of the Silvine their hotels might appear shabby in Oliver Wingate's eyes. But not run-down. Had Martin's father, perhaps made nervous by his son's behaviour, felt the need to entrench himself with a stake in their business by way of insurance? Hah! That made sense! She felt a resurgence of her lost confidence.

The waiter came for her plate. She ordered ice cream. I was hungry. That's why I went to pieces. She signed to the man to return. She asked him to make the ice cream a double. A parfait.

"*Avec noisettes?*"

"*Oui.*" Some nuts, too. And a small *café*.

It was amazing what could be achieved on a full stomach, she decided as she paid the bill and set off for Le Septre. She walked with a lighter step.

When she arrived there was no one about except the desk clerk. She went straight up to the family apartment. Turned on the lights. Standing inside the door she looked round, taking stock for the second time in weeks. Differently though. Velvet upholstery. Chinese carpet. An impressive, glittering chandelier. No wonder her parents treated her as a child! Children live with their parents in middle aged comfort.

She took off her jacket and flung it down on a chair arm.

152

Martin's ring fell out and rolled across the floor. She picked it up. Put it on the mantel. She felt it belonged there. With the family. So, do I move out when Neil leaves hospital? She felt a sense of urgency. Her mind registered that she had said Neil. That the name had taken her one step along the trail towards independence. She considered the fact that Neil might not be back at work for a long time. Might never work again. Living with him meant involving him. So, she had to live separately, and yet not too far away for that was the nature of hotel business, to be at hand.

A solution slanted into her mind. What about the attics!

The attics at the Hotel le Sceptre comprised a series of smallish rooms, originally servants quarters. Their dormer windows faced the front. Julie had not been up there for years. She would look at them with a view to conversion. But at what cost? Before any money was spent she had to find fifty thousand pounds.

I will sleep on it, she decided. She picked up her things and went off to her room. She was in her dressing gown and ready for bed when Delia came back from the hospital. She heard her moving about and came to greet her. Delia did not hear her footsteps on the thick carpet. She was standing in the middle of the big drawing room staring into space, looking desperately unhappy.

"Hello," said Julie.

Her mother's face lit up and she came forward eagerly. "You saw Martin?"

Julie recognised in the change of manner, the bright eyes, how badly Delia wanted this marriage. She didn't feel resentful. Or bitter. Only confident that the strength of her mother's wishes had to be matched with honesty.

"I saw Martin," she said briskly, "and also Antonia."

Delia saw the change from daughter to businesswoman and it startled her. She didn't seem to know how to reply.

Julie said in a matter-of-fact voice, "He's living with Antonia. She is very much in love with him, as I am not. I've made it clear to him, and his father, and incidentally also to Antonia, that he's out of my life for good."

"Julie!" Delia put a hand to the side of her face and

153

closed her eyes as though she could not bear to look at this new daughter who was tearing her life apart. "I don't understand you," she wailed. "I don't understand you. This will kill your father."

"It won't because we won't tell him," Julie said. "I'm sorry I have to bother you with it, but I can't have you hearing from other people." She wished she had been dressed in business clothes instead of a fluffy dressing gown. A daughter in a fluffy dressing gown. "What I need to know now is how Neil came to borrow fifty thousand pounds from Oliver Wingate and what arrangements there are for paying it back. I know you're not *au fait* with the running of the business, but as this borrowing was connected with my marrying Martin, it's something I think you must know about. You must tell me the whole story."

Delia looked at her as though she was an alien being from outer space.

"Let's sit down," Julie suggested and gestured towards Delia's favourite seat, on the sofa.

Delia sat down, bonelessly, in a heap. She looked at Julie with frightened eyes then stood up again, took off her coat and laid it over a chair arm. Julie again indicated the seat. Obedient as a child, Delia collapsed again.

"Well?"

"There were no arrangements for paying that money back, dear," Delia said. "It wasn't your father's idea to borrow it. Oliver insisted on putting the money in. Into the business. He has what he calls a big cash flow. That was what the amalgamation was about. He thought our hotels were running down. Neil said we didn't have a big cash flow," Delia added, trusting and innocent, "so if the buildings had to be decorated, then Oliver had to pay for it."

"He persuaded Neil they were running down?" Julie watched the drifting shadows in her mother's eyes and recognised that the transition from daughter to woman-in-charge was not going to be difficult.

"I suppose so," Delia agreed uncertainly. "I do know he wasn't entirely . . . . But anyway, as I said, Oliver convinced him it would add to the hotel's property value, and he

154

produced the money, and . . ." Delia's voice trailed away. Then she began again in a rush, beseeching, "It was a family arrangement. You were going to marry Martin."

"And you were using me as collateral, that's the truth of it, isn't it?"

"I don't know what you mean, Julie. Don't look at me like that," Delia wailed.

"You wanted me to marry Martin so that I could keep an eye on the business." She thought, and Martin was removing me from the scene so I would not be able to.

Delia looked harrassed.

"Let's talk about money," Julie said. "I've had to take charge and you've got to accept that. You've got to stop making it difficult for me. Oliver Wingate persuaded you and Neil it was a family arrangement? I do see that in those circumstances there would be a problem in the event that the amalgamation didn't go through."

Delia was frightened now. Julie could see it in her eyes. "It has to go through, Julie. We can't find fifty thousand pounds."

It was clear this was not the moment to tell her mother she had asked Wingate to withdraw. She cast around for something to say that would put her mother's mind at ease. If she was frightened she was going to upset Neil. "I will find the money," she said.

"Oh Julie!" Delia was pathetically grateful. So easily taken in.

"How was Neil?"

"Why are you calling him Neil?"

"It's the new me. How was he?"

Delia's face lit up. "He's out of intensive care. But frail. Dreadfully frail." She looked at Julie with pleading eyes. Pleading with her to make everything perfect as it was before. "If anything were to go wrong now . . ."

"Nothing will go wrong." She dropped the executive-in-charge manner with relief. "He's bound to be frail. He's been very ill. Would you like me to make you a Horlicks drink?"

"That would be kind." Her mother hauled herself off the sofa. Looked at Julie uncertainly. "You're not yourself tonight, dear," she ventured.

"I'm quite safe." She smiled. "As I said, I've found a new me." And I don't especially like this new me, she thought. She remembered Moira saying she thought human beings could be provoked into anything. I have been provoked into being a bully, she thought. I trust it's only temporary.

To her surprise, she lost consciousness immediately and wakened feeling refreshed. Delia, apparently considering herself absolved from all worry, wanted her breakfast in bed. Julie was thankful. She sent for Anatole. She told him briefly that she had asked Wingate to consider the cancellation of the amalgamation of their three hotels with the Silvine. "That should go some distance towards calming the atmosphere," she said.

"You have authority to do this?" He was astonished.

"No," she said, "just between you and me. Don't tell the others that. I'm feeling my way."

His dark brown eyes lit up, he opened his mouth to speak then appearing to be overcome with emotion he grasped her hand. "Thank you for telling me, Julie. Thank you."

"Set the rumour going, but be sure to say nothing is definite."

Anatole nodded. "I know the staff would like me to say we're all behind you, and that we wish you well."

"Thank you."

"How is Bettine?"

"She is very comfortable and delighted to be here." Anatole grinned. "She is not in the habit of staying at such a hotel as this."

"Well, good. That's great. So everyone's pleased. I'll try to get up to see her."

"Thank you for the flowers."

"Did someone arrange them?"

"Yes. Melusine. They are beautiful."

Within an hour word had swept through the building. Everyone was smiling. Everyone wanted to come to Julie's office and tell her personally how glad they were that things were going to remain unchanged. She had wanted to immerse herself in work but the work had to wait. She was touched and flattered by the reaction of the staff. And

156

privately disturbed that Oliver Wingate had such a reputation. In the privacy of her office they told her of rumours that had not come her way. His name was synonomous with change. For modernisation. With quick deals. The staff had been afraid of take-over bids. They had felt unsafe.

"Why did nobody tell me these things?" she asked.

"You were going to marry his son. We thought, we hoped, you would keep a balance."

She had not realised how her engagement had alienated her from them.

"We were very pleased," confided Anatole, "when we heard the engagement was off. They telephoned me at home."

Julie understood. Of course nobody would speak up against the man who was to be her father-in-law. But she was chastened by what had happened.

In the afternoon Oliver Wingate called.

"I've spoken to the boy," he said, curtly dispensing with preliminaries. "You can tell your father that in the circumstances, due to the way you've treated Martin, and with regard to Neil's state of health, we're going to withdraw from the amalgamation.

"Thank you, Mr. Wingate. I'm grateful for your early decision."

"I shall want my fifty thousand pounds repaid, though. And fast."

"Of course. It will be paid, but I must ask you to give me a little time."

Julie made an appointment with her father's bank manager for the following day.

It was one thing to take over the family, she discovered, but quite another to deal with the banks.

Monsieur le Blanc was a small man with thick black hair and a bald patch on the top of his head. The enormous executive desk at which he sat made him appear smaller. He indicated that she take a chair opposite.

"What can I do for you, M'selle?"

He listened courteously to her request for a loan, then

without answering directly asked, "Your father is still in hospital?"

"Yes. That's why I have had to come to you. His doctors won't allow anyone to worry him." Watching his face, she saw creeping over it a mask of suspicion and doubt. She felt chilled.

"May I ask what the loan is for?" He leaned forward, forearms on the desk, fixing her with his very dark and piercing eyes.

She told him. "I have to pay the money back. Mr Wingate wants it immediately."

"And you have broken off your engagement?"

"Yes."

He stared down at the table. Julie felt the chill intensify.

"You have said the hotel amalgamation is off."

"Yes."

He leaned forward and said in a kind way, almost kind and certainly suitable for speaking to young people, "Wouldn't it be better to wait until your father comes out of hospital?"

She swallowed. Her mouth felt dry. "Mr Wingate wants his money now. We have no idea when my father will come out of hospital."

Again there was a pause, longer this time.

"And you are in charge? Your father has put you in charge?"

"My father is too ill to deal with any business affairs. I am in charge because I have been working with him since I left school and I know the running of the hotels."

"You put yourself in charge?"

"My father was in intensive care." Her voice had begun to sound hollow. "You must understand he cannot make decisions of any kind."

When the man did not immediately reply she added, "He would expect me to take over. Of course he would. There is no one else."

"You have a lot of authority?"

She didn't know how to answer that.

"Assuming you had a lot of authority, nonetheless you didn't know about this loan?"

Her throat felt dry. The palms of her hands were hot. He was behaving as though they were in a court of law. He the barrister for the prosecution, she the prisoner in the dock. She felt the confidence she had so painstakingly built up drain away. She realised she had lost credulity. She tried to find excuses. She was involved with her approaching wedding. Temporarily otherwise engaged.

"But you work at Le Septre," he said, "and from time to time you work at both the London hotel and the Swiss one. You must know a good deal about the running of them. I fail to understand why you would not have known about plans for refurbishing."

"I can only think my father felt I had enough on my plate," she replied. She recognised it as a weak excuse. And she had delivered it without confidence for that had been running down ever since those intense dark eyes had first looked into hers across the desk. In the silence that followed she faced up to the fact that even when you are familiar with the work concerned you cannot step, overnight, into another person's shoes.

She went to their accountants. She told them her mother was worried about repayment of the Wingate money. "Was she right to worry?" Julie asked. Or could they pay it back if the amalgamation did not go through?

"Let's wait until your father is better," they said.

She made an appointment with the solicitors and suffered a re-enactment of the other two scenes. She was an unknown, and what was more, she had left her family with an expensive wedding on their hands. They did not trust her, that was the truth of it. They had no proof of the fact that responsibility for running of the businesses had reverted to her.

It was one thing to take charge with the staff who knew her, she realised, quite another to be accepted by tough businessmen. She walked all the way back, along one street after another, hoping to tire herself out emotionally. Walking promoted calm. Half an hour later she arrived back at the hotel feeling very frightened indeed.

There was plenty of work to do, for that she was grateful.

She called in Melusine and spent an hour dictating letters. She remembered that she had again forgotten lunch. She asked for tea and scones to be sent up to Bettine in her sick room on the second floor and went up to visit her. The doctor had been. She was to stay in bed at least another week.

"Don't apologise," said Julie. "We're delighted to have you. Call it selfishness. We need Anatole." Bettine did not look at all well. A muscular disease was developing. It didn't bear thinking about. Other people have troubles, she thought. We are not alone.

She went back to her office. Melusine said, "You're worried, Julie. Is there anything I can do to help?"

She recognised that Melusine, and perhaps the rest of the staff as well, had not been taken in by the cheerful manner she had adopted. She had been aware of curious looks. "Thanks, Mel," she said. "I'm tired, that's all."

She imagined her secretary saying in reply to questions, "She's distinctly worried. I could tell," and word would fly round. The staff would start worrying again. She thought it best to remove her anxiety from their gaze. She asked for a meal to be sent up later for Delia and herself then went up to her father's study. She made a conscious decision to go right through his filing cabinet. If there were private papers, then too bad. She had to know what had been going on.

It was a very long and boring process. Unsatisfactory in the extreme for most of the letters she read were on matters familiar to her. She began to think Neil had no secrets from her and felt angry with the bank manager for treating her as a Jonny-come-lately.

She was relieved to hear her mother arriving. She tidied up the desk and went to meet her. Delia was smiling, humming to herself as she crossed the drawing room. "Your father is delighted to hear you've been able to pay the money back," she said. "He's going to try to persuade the staff to let you see him. He wants to talk to you about what you've done. He wanted you to tell him all about it."

Julie said through stiff lips, "I thought you of all people would apply the rule of not talking business to the patient."

"But this isn't business," Delia cried, tossing her handbag down on a chair, stretching luxuriously. "This is good news, which is quite different. You should see the change in him! His eyes are brighter and his colour is better already."

"I'm glad." She wished she could run away. Jump out of the window. Get drunk. Why had she not foreseen that her hare-brained mother would do this!

"He's going to try to persuade the doctor to allow you in tomorrow."

Of course her father would want to see her now. He wasn't likely to be taken in by her mother's glib report that their troubles were at an end. Julie said the first thing that came into her head, "Moira has invited me to go to Italy to her villa for a few days."

"How can you go?"

"I'm in charge. Those in charge make the rules. I wasn't aware I could see Neil when I accepted the invitation. And anyway, you did say he hasn't got permission to see me – yet."

"But he will get it. I'm sure."

"He probably won't," said Julie.

"What's the matter, Julie? You're so unlike yourself. Neil. Delia. I don't know what's come over you," her mother complained. "What is the matter, dear?"

"Nothing a day or two away won't alleviate. I'm tired." And she was. She felt too tired to go on. She went to the window and looked down at the traffic crawling along the street below because she could not bear to look at her mother, at the trust in her heart which was showing as pure light in her eyes. She felt crucified by her mother's faith in her.

There was a tap at the door. Julie turned. Went with relief to open it. Jacques was there, ready to wheel in their meal. She thanked him and stood back while he proceeded to the dining room. She didn't offer to deal with it herself. She needed the break to give Delia's thoughts time to re-form.

They didn't. "When are you thinking of going?"

Julie spoke off the top of her head. "The day after

161

tomorrow. Or maybe tomorrow evening, if I can get things shipshape. A long weekend."

"But you've said you're so busy. Terribly busy, you said." Delia was puzzled, as well she might be, Julie thought.

"Anatole's return has made a difference. By the way, do go and see Bettine. She's in room sixteen. Why don't you nip down now. I've got a phone call to make before we eat."

"I don't know," said Delia, looking bewildered.

"Go and see Bettine. Just spend ten minutes with her. She would be grateful."

Delia heaved a sigh, then went.

Julie returned to the study and called Moira's apartment.

"Wonderful!" Moira exclaimed. "I will try to get a flight late tomorrow afternoon. That will give us three full days."

Julie put the receiver down. She had no conscience about running away. She must not see her father until she had worked something out.

That night in bed she tossed and turned. There wasn't much to work out, she thought, as the hours ticked slowly by. When she went to see her father she was going to have to tell him she had changed her mind and would marry Martin. Only she couldn't do it tomorrow. Nor the next day. Nor the next. She remembered what Greg had said about being cured and free. Since a short time ago, now that it was too late, she had been free. But fate had sliced that decision through its vulnerable centre and turned her round to face Martin again. Just like Greg, she had been cured when it was too late. She thought of the irony of it.

She had no doubt Martin would have her. After all, she said to herself, he has a great deal to gain. And by Antonia's admission he could still have her as a mistress. His father would forget what she had said to him, and forgive her, she was certain of that.

At three o'clock she rose, put on a wrap and went down to the kitchen to make a hot drink. She took it into the drawing room. The engagement ring Martin had given her lay where she had placed in on the mantel. She looked at it with loathing then slipped it on the third finger of her left hand, seeing clearly and with despair what it signified.

A lifetime of humiliation on the one hand, and a lifetime of fight on the other, for she would never allow Oliver Wingate full control of what once had been their family's hotels. Never. On behalf of the staff as well as her family, she would fight that to the bitter end. And as for Martin and me, since it is to be a marriage in name only, then I will be within my rights in refusing to have anything to do with his antique business, she said to herself. His father cannot prevent me working in the hotels. That is what Neil wanted from the marriage. He shall have his safety valve. There is no other way.

She thought of Antonia. Her humiliation will be no greater than mine, she decided, and wept for them both.

Chapter Ten

Moira prowled into the big salon wearing one of her own creations, a silk trouser suit, jet black and gilded by a jangling collection of gold chains. "We will have no trouble raising the money." She glanced at Julie in her pale blue jumper and cotton jeans. "You think I am overdressed? Of course I am." She looked down at her feet, at the black velvet slippers heavily embroidered in gold. "We are going out to dinner. I like to be noticed."

"You would be noticed even without all that glamour," Julie told her, savouring the picture of a glamorous chatelaine in her equally glamorous villa. "I'm sorry but I haven't brought anything smart. I hope we're not going to a very posh restaurant. You may be ashamed of me. When I came last time I was defiant. I brought some clothes meant for my honeymoon. Goodness knows who I thought was going to look at them."

Greg did, she remembered. Greg saw her new honeymoon bikini. As well as the elegant silk trousers; her new and oh so extravagant Italian silk blouse with the little pearl buttons. Her pretty shoes. That was how she had dressed when Greg took her out to dinner. Greg, who had gone off to Geneva 'on business' with another woman. She looked down at the engagement ring on her left hand. She had brought it with her as an aid in convincing herself of what she must now do.

"And ended up wearing them in the hill towns?"

She jumped as Moira spoke.

Moira looked at her with a droll expression.

"*Cherie*, you do go a long way away sometimes."

"Sorry." Julie flushed. "No. Actually, when I was driving

164

around I lived in one T-shirt and one pair of jeans. Today when I rushed away I wasn't thinking about clothes at all. My thoughts were totally taken up with making certain everything was going to work while I was away, thankfully out of reach of the telephone." At least she hadn't had to calm her mother down. Delia in her fool's paradise, whilst disappointed that it was not possible for Julie to talk to her father, was eventually resigned to the fact that she needed a few days in the sun; felt Julie had earned it in finding the money to repay Wingate. She shivered.

Moira wagged an admonishing finger at her. "There is no point in my taking you away if you are going to bring your troubles as baggage. I will find someone to loan you money," she said, overflowing with goodwill. "No problem. I am glad you have confided in me. It is not a large sum. In today's terms, I mean. I am surprised there's such a fuss about it. I'd have expected a man with three hotels to be able to raise that amount unless his business was already in a bit of a mess."

She saw the stiffening of Julie's features and broke off but the seed of doubt had been sown. No, not sown. Brought to flower. Hadn't Martin said that morning after she broke off the engagement, when he brought the roses, "Your father's not much of a businessman." She had overridden his words at the time, forgotten them in her indignation over his saying their hotels were down-at-heel. Now she saw the very real possibility that Neil could be in trouble. Could have brought Wingate in to help. But at the expense of changing the whole aspect of his hotels? She saw the amalgamation in the form of a compromise.

She thought with a flash of insight, this is what Martin's father meant when he said he would break Neil. One does not break a person in his position with a debt of fifty thousand pounds. She felt cold, and all at once very frightened.

"Of course they will need collateral," Moira said.

Julie started as though stabbed with a pin. "I can't get collateral without talking to my father."

"Is any of the property in your name?"

Julie went to the big window and stood looking out on

165

the Bay of Salerno that was spread out before them with lights twinkling round the shore and the moon drenching the water with silver.

"No collateral?" Moira came to stand beside her, hand on hip, frowning.

"Not the kind I would have authority to use. You must understand, Moira, my parents treated me as an adult with regard to the work I was doing, but not in other ways. Yes, there is property in my name but I couldn't raise money on it without my father's sanction. Everything comes back to that. Nothing can be done without reference to him. And his doctors won't allow him to talk about business."

Julie looked down at the cotton jumper and trim trousers she wore. "I'm sorry to let you down by looking so ordinary." She felt like a wren standing in the shadow of a peacock. "I may as well say it out loud. I believe I'm going to need all my smart clothes, after all. The wedding dress as well. I can't see any way out of this dilemma except to eat humble pie and marry Martin."

"This," said Moira indignantly, "is medieval. Young women are not sold into marriage these days. I mean it, *cherie*. That is what you're talking about. Your father has been a fool," she said bluntly. "He cannot expect you to pay for his mistakes."

"I'm sure he doesn't. It's his life we're talking about, Moira," said Julie soberly. "I find myself in a position where I'm responsible for his life. And I am the cause of his inability to repay. He didn't borrow the money. He allowed Wingate to put it into the business because he had complete faith that I would marry Martin and keep his affairs safe."

"But he didn't ask your permission."

"No." Julie said ruefully, "He couldn't, could he? I mean, one doesn't. He didn't do anything wrong. It only became wrong – as you so quaintly put it, medieval – when I decided not to marry Martin." It was the first time she had actually put the matter into words. They took the sting out of her resentment. Her father's manoeuvring took on normality she had not recognised before.

166

"This man Wingate," said Moira passionately, "is a bastard." *Bâtard.* She spat the word. "And your father is a fool." She saw Julie's startled expression and added, "I am sorry to be so insulting, but that is the truth of it."

Julie thought, it is so, what she says. Hearing it spoken out loud was a little like having a boil lanced. "I will think of something," Moira said, but she spoke without her usual confidence. "Anyway, you do not have to marry that Martin. That liar. Never. I will think of something," she said again.

She went with a light step to the drinks cupboard. "Let us forget and relax. That's what we came here for. To relax. A drink first, and then we will go out to dinner. I have a favourite restaurant. It's late, but they will always find me a table." She closed the cupboard door and stood erect again. "Perhaps we will dispense with the drink. It will be a better ambience there. Two women alone in a villa! That is not very exciting. And as I said, it is late. I hadn't noticed how time had run on."

Julie recognised then that Moira's coming to the villa with her was a sacrifice of a kind. Moira the gregarious, the flamboyant, who loved to show off her clothes, would certainly have preferred a house party. She felt a deep sense of gratitude.

"Come, pick up a wrap or a jacket," Moira said. "It can get cool in the evening at this time of year although I have to say it is exceptionally warm tonight." She wriggled to indicate her discomfort. "This top is sticking to my back. I am perspiring. I hope we're not going to have a thunder storm."

Julie glanced anxiously out the window. The moonlight had gone behind clouds. The bay was a black expanse edged with pinpoints of gold. She went to her room to pick up a wrap. Moira was standing in the hall waiting for her. "Here is your key. Put it in your bag. You never know."

"What?"

Moira shrugged. "You may want to walk on the beach. I may want to come home earlier. Who knows. One should always be free to do one's own thing."

167

"Of course." Julie thought about the key Moira hid in the garden for her friends who came by sea. The perfect hostess.

They left the car on the roof and went down the winding road where Julie had so recently walked with Greg. When they had gone several hundred metres Moira pointed to some steps in the hillside. "We can go up here," she said. "These steps are very steep but they are quicker than the ones further down. What do you think?" She waited for Julie's reply.

Julie looked across the road. "I don't mind the steepness."

They crossed and went up to where the retaining wall split allowing for the steps to be hewn into the mountainside. Julie took the lead. The steps were narrow but they were partially lit by tiny lights set in the granite. Small flowering cacti grew on either side and here and there bigger bushes with lush blossoms leaned over their path.

"This restaurant has a view of the lights of the town as well as the sea," Moira said as they climbed. She turned to look out over the water. "I do hope we don't have a storm. It is so hot! You are hot, *cherie*?"

"Not especially." The sensation of cold that had crept in when Moira commented that fifty thousand pounds was not such a vast sum for a hotelier to find had stayed with her. She told herself she was nervy because she was hungry. She would feel better for some food. She had scarcely eaten all day. Going without food seemed to have become a habit. Moira had eaten a good lunch but she had toyed with hers.

"Have you experienced an Italian coastal thunder storm?" Moira was puffing up behind her.

She paused, also looking out over the sea. "No."

"These mountains are noted for thunderstorms. But luckily, they don't last too long. The length of a good meal," said Moira casually. "And they can be very spectacular viewed from up here. I could almost wish one for you. You would find it an experience." A low growl of thunder came out of the darkness. "Ah!" said Moira, not altogether with satisfaction. "I wish it for you but it is not so much fun when the lights go out."

168

Julie had gained on her. She turned to say, "I think I might see a really spectacular thunderstrom as a recreation. Even a solace."

"Let's wish it on ourselves, then." Moira looked out over the darkened bay and cried dramatically, "Come, storm! Come, thunder! Give us a bit of excitement."

Julie laughed. By the time they came to a little plateau and Moira was saying, "We are here," it was clear that whether she had invoked the storm or not, it was coming. They stopped to gaze in awe as forked lightning swept round the curve of the mountain above and ahead of them, lighting up the rock formations eerily. A clap of thunder followed, as yet far out to sea. Ahead of them were the arched windows of the brightly-lit restaurant. She could see the heads of the diners. Waiters hovering.

"We should have brought coats and umbrellas," she said.

"Coats and umbrellas would do us no good in the kind of storm that's coming." Moira stepped after her onto the grass. "Don't you know an umbrella could attract the lightning? Anyway, it won't last." Suddenly they became aware that fat raindrops were falling. "Hurry," urged Moira and began to run. Julie sped after her.

They were stepping into cloisters. Julie looked round. She felt a prick of memory. Memory became certainty. She had a feeling of *déjà-vu* accompanied by an unbearable stab of pain.

"What's the matter?" Moira looked round.

"I came here with Greg. But we came up another path. And there were tables on the grass. It looked different. I didn't recognise it." She should have known Moira's favourite restaurant would also be Greg's.

"It is a good place to eat," said Moira complacently. "The best. I am sorry not to introduce you to somewhere new but you would not get better food anywhere." A wind came with great force from across the garden, lashing the colonnade, sweeping across the stone blocked floor.

"My God!" exclaimed Moira. "Run." They sped towards the brightly lit doorway then turned, looking back. "Another moment and we'd have been soaked to the skin."

Julie thought she had never seen such rain. It hurled itself across the floor, hit the wall and ran back like an ebbing tide. Waiters came forward, welcoming Moira warmly. *"Buon giorno."* They dispensed compliments, recognised Julie with extravagant cries of pleasure. *"Avanti!* The rain! How lucky you were!" Of course a table would be found for them. It was late, certainly, but never too late for the Signora. The head waiter lamented that she had not been here often enough.

"They miss me." Moira was flattered. Her dark eyes glowed.

Julie was watching the rain. It beat against the windows. Poured down them like a river in flood. People were screwing round in their chairs, staring at it.

The waiter glanced at Julie then spoke to Moira in fast Italian. Moira looked dismayed. She pointed to the corner of the restaurant that jutted out towards the view. The man nodded. He spoke again in Italian, shrugging. Julie followed his eyes. In that corner all the tables were full.

"What's the matter, Moira?" she asked.

"Nothing, *cherie.* Nothing at all. We are to wait just a moment because some people are leaving. Then we will take their table, over there." She nodded towards the corner.

Julie's eyes flicked round the room. "There are several empty tables in the centre," she said.

"We want to sit in the corner. By the window. You will like to look over the water." Moira was adamant, though there was nothing to see. The windows were deeply recessed. The walls must have been more than a foot thick. "It will stop in a moment," Moira said, though patently it would not. Julie assumed Moira's favourite table was in the corner. A party of four began to push their chairs back.

"Ah!" said Moira with satisfaction. "They are going."

The head waiter snapped out an order. Two minions hurried over. They began to clear the table and brush the cloth.

Moira went ahead and took the chair in the corner. She had her back to the window. "You sit there, Julie, where you can watch the storm," she said, pointing. The waiter pulled out her chair. As she settled into it a great clap of thunder sounded directly overhead. The lights went out. There were tiny high-pitched shrieks, a rattle of excited chatter, then comparative silence.

"We will have to manage with candles," said Moira exultantly. "Two women together do not present a very romantic picture. The candles will help."

Julie recognised again Moira's great kindness. That she was unaccustomed to holidaying *à deux*, with a woman. Now she saw why there was always a key left in the garden for friends. She was once again aware, guiltily, of her ordinary clothes. She felt she had let Moira down.

She looked out of the window, at the blackness and the rain on the glass. Another flash of lightning came, vivid in the black sky, darting through the room, evoking more high-pitched shrieks. Candles emerged from the darkness conveyed by white cuffs and movement. Black-clad waiters busy in the darkness. Gradually the restaurant settled down. The menu came and they ordered.

"*La carta dei vini*," said Moira and was handed the wine list. "No one will be going home for a while. Except those who came by car. The steps will be a torrent. Flood water comes quickly from the hills. They cannot hold it because of the rock. We may as well settle down and enjoy ourselves. What will you have, Julie? You must, of course, have fish. Either fish soup or fish for a main course. In the coastal towns they do not allow foreigners to eat anything else."

"Will the kitchen be in working order, since there's no power?"

Moira scoffed. "They are accustomed to power failures. They are prepared. It happens frequently, you understand."

Julie said, "I'll be very happy to oblige by ordering fish soup."

Forked lightning darted into the room, swept round the walls like lethal, golden snakes. A concerted shriek arose. Julie swung round viewing the pandemonium with curiosity and amusement. Women jumped out of their seats, picked up their wraps, entreated their men to take them home.

"Such nerves!" remarked Moira disdainfully. "They are

in the most spectacular site in the town and they want to run away and hide."

Julie thought it was the Italian temperament. Moira was subject to quick passions. She remembered her passion back at the villa when she had called Oliver Wingate a bastard. Her father a fool. She remembered Greg's version. Men like Wingate eat your father's type for breakfast. She shook her thoughts away. Wasn't she supposed to be forgetting her troubles?

"We have been having thunderstorms since the beginning of time," boasted Moira, stout in her defence of them, "and no building has ever been struck. Why would the church build their monasteries on such promontories as this if they were going to be struck by lightning? This is an old monastery, did you know?"

"I guessed. It makes an excellent restaurant."

People continued to leave. The hustle of their anxiety filled the room. A woman stopped at their table. They both looked up. Julie felt a prickle of recognition, then it went.

"Ah! Pauline!" exclaimed Moira. "Sit down." She signed to a passing waiter to bring a chair. They waited until she was settled. "Julie, I want you to meet my friend." She pronounced her name Paulina in the Italian way. "Pauline, Julie."

The woman held out her hand and Julie extended hers.

"Why are you dining alone?" asked Moira. "One woman alone is just a little more sad than two women alone."

Pauline smiled. "I was not alone. I was dining with Greg. He, what would you say? Dumped me? He is worried about *Neptuna*. He left me with *il conto*." She looked ruefully at Julie. Julie's face had gone stiff, her eyes glazed. "Such a gentleman!" she said, but with affection so that it was clear to Moira and Julie she did not mind being left with the bill.

Julie looked at Moira's face behind the candle flame and knew with startled certainty why she had insisted on this table. Knew that the earnest discussion with the waiters had been about the fact that Greg was in the dining room with another woman. Greg, who had brought her here and intimated to them that romance was in the air. Who had sanctioned the presentation of a hibiscus blossom. She saw that was why Moira had seated her with her back to the room. So that she would not see him with this woman Pauline. She knew from the way Moira avoided her eyes this was so.

"Where are you staying, Pauline?"

"On *Neptuna*." Then she spoke in an aside, in Italian. Julie recognised the word *vigile* and knew she was talking about the police. When she heard *Génève* she recognised with stunning certainty why the woman looked familiar. It was she who had slipped into Greg's car in the Paris street as Julie was about to enter Moira's salon. She remembered not only her face, seen dimly now in the flickering candlelight, but her long legs and long fair hair. One of Greg's girls.

"We only arrived this afternoon," Pauline said. "Incidentally, you may have to give us a bed tonight."

"*Si*. Of course. Where is *Neptuna*?" Clearly Moira was embarrassed but she failed to convey this to Pauline who merely looked puzzled.

"Below the Villa Rosa. We came into the main beach in the tender because we didn't know you were in residence."

"A pity."

"And Greg didn't batten down the hatches. When we left there was no sign of a storm coming up. I hope, for his sake, the lightning has gone away before he reaches the boat. He's going to be soaked. We don't want him electrocuted as well."

"Don't say such things," snapped Moira. "It is a joke in very bad taste."

Julie shot her a startled look. Moira avoided her eyes. Oh hell, Julie thought, this is an impossible situation. A waiter brought the soup. The shellfish danced before her eyes. Dimly she was aware that Moira was pouring wine into her glass and calling in a tense, brittle voice for another glass for their guest. She looked hot and discomfited. She pulled the silk material away from her shoulders as she had done at the villa. "It is hot in here. Airless," she said. Her eyes darted to Julie, then to Pauline, then back to Julie.

173

There was only one thing for it, Julie decided. She would absent herself for a few moments. Give Moira an opportunity to explain the awkwardness. A flicker of lightning, weak with distance, caught her eye. Thunder faintly rolled out over the sea. The windows were no longer runnng with water. The storm was going away. She pushed her chair back, picked up her bag and rose.

Moira and Pauline looked up.

"Excuse me," she said. "I won't be long." She laid her napkin on the table and slipped away, stepping between the tables, aware of their eyes on her back. Once outside the door she felt the tension drift away. She started along the cloisters. The stone flagging was very wet but the water was running off on to the grass. She wondered how long she should give them. She thought about what Moira had to impart. Greg has been leading this girl on. Be careful what you say, Pauline. She fancies herself in love with him. Do you mind staying at an hotel? It would be embarrassing . . . Two women, in the same villa, both in love with Greg. Certainly you cannot sleep with him there. Julie is my friend. Not, of course, such an old friend as you but still, my friend.

She moved back towards the door. It wasn't easy to see the diners. The little pools of candlelight did not illuminate their faces. With the cloister lights extinguished the darkness here was comforting.

Suddenly the lights came on. She saw Moira and Pauline with heads thrown back, laughing as though at some tremendous joke. They lifted their glasses simultaneously, and smiling at each other drank some secret toast.

Chapter Eleven

I have been humiliated enough, Julie said to herself as she headed across the grass. A tall lamp standard showed her where the steps lay. I am opting out. Taking the easy road. Is this my mother emerging in me? Then I may come to understand her better. I have been made a fool of by my parents, by Martin, incidentally by his father, and now by Greg. I have the key to the villa. I am going to run away.

She came to the steps and stood looking down the steep hillside with dismay. The narrow rock walkway had become the base of a running stream. Where was the water coming from? She looked behind her but there was only the blackness of rock cliff. Then she remembered Moira saying flood water came back quickly from the hills on account of their rock formation.

In the brightly lit restaurant less than fifty feet away she could see the heads. The back of Moira's head in the corner window nearest to where she was standing, and less clearly, Pauline's profile. She turned swiftly away and contemplated the water. Shook her head. Turned back. There was a road behind the restaurant that would take her down into the bay. Last time she was here she had seen diners going out there to their cars. She would take that. In the circumstances, the road would be safer now.

She walked across the soaking grass, her feet squelching. She skirted the cloisters. The lights went only half way. As far as the powder room. Beyond, a black wall of darkness. She would have to find a way through here. She put one foot down and tested the ground before moving her weight forward. She held her arms out in front, feeling for obstacles. There were none. She gained confidence. Moved faster, taking her weight with her first foot. When it failed to strike solid ground she hurtled forward, head first, with a shriek of fright, into a waterway.

She scrambled back with water seeping through her clothes, soaking down her front and all along her legs. She didn't want to find out what she had fallen into. There was no moon. No chink in the blackness. Perhaps it was not possible to get round to the car park from this side of the building. She turned back. Remembered the other set of steps up which she had climbed with Greg. She would have to find them now.

She went back along the edge of the cloisters and skirted the front of the building looking warily in through the arched windows. She could see Moira and Pauline. They were both looking towards the door. She felt guilty. And foolish. Hoist with my own petard, she thought and tried to laugh about it. Her wet trousers sucked at her ankles.

Now she had reached the opposite corner of the building. The darkness was total. She could not remember where she and Greg had come out. If I topple over, she thought, it is a long fall. She went back, past the windows. Pauline was alone now. Moira must have gone to look for her. Again, she experienced that stab of guilt. She came to the steps. At least here there were guiding lights. She was so wet now a bit more water was not going to make any difference.

She went down one step, then two, then three. The lights were there, a comfort in the darkness, but she could no longer see the steps, only the water, glittering as it ran past a globe of light. It spun round her ankles at great speed, camouflaging the shape of the hewn rock. She took her bearings from either side. Now that she needed the lights badly they were too far apart. And too small. But they did serve as indicators, giving her the courage to go on.

A sudden rush of water hit her, spinning up waist high, soaking her to the skin. She cried out in shock and fear. Floundered. Of course the flood would gather speed as it descended. This was madness. But she couldn't go back. Not now, soaked to the skin and with no alternate route except through the restaurant.

176

She grasped a handful of some tough rock plant. It might have been a cactus but luckily was not. She clung to it while she plucked up the courage to go on. She eased her bottom onto the jutting rock beside which the plant was growing and from this insubstantial point of safety looked down at where the water dashed past into darkness. She assessed the possibility of the lights going out again. Why should they? The storm had gone on its way.

Ahead, by the light of one of those little globes she thought she perceived one of the narrow railings she had noticed as they ascended. She remembered they had been set on awkward corners where the path turned sharply. She eased herself down off her perch, stretched out one leg and found a foothold on the steps. Reaching out very carefully, bracing her calves against the weight of the water, she felt for the step below. This was going to take hours. She found the submerged edge of the next step with her toe, the abutment with her heel. She set her foot down firmly then braced herself and took another.

It wasn't going to take hours. It wasn't that difficult. So long as she didn't turn round. Or trip. So long as she watched the corners. So long as she didn't make a false move.

It was not a section of railing she had seen. Instead, it was a jutting rock with cactus growing close. She was almost relieved. Those few moments of optimism had given her time to try herself out. With the trying she had gathered confidence. Now she knew she could keep going. Her spirits rose a fraction.

Slowly, and very, very carefully, she continued to make her way down the rock face. There were few handholds and those she saw she distrusted. She had been lucky with that first plant. She hoped she wouldn't have to take another chance. Progress was easier now. The water, that might in an ideal situation have cascaded in a steady flow, leapt and bounced and splashed. Sometimes, on a sharp bend where the steps veered off to the left it took a short cut and flew off in a miniature waterfall leaving a dozen steps clear. She found a system of balance that took in the weight of the water against her calves and the tug of the material of her trousers, but it failed to work when suddenly the rock face became steeper, or levelled out.

Left foot foward, feel the edge, heel in. Caught by an increase of the water's speed she rocked on her feet. She was losing her balance! She looked round wildy for one of those dangerous handholds and failing to find one, sat down. The water sped up the back of her neck, shot over her shoulders. She staggered to her feet, breathless and frightened.

And then the lights went out.

Sheer nightmare! A blaze of lightning fled across the sky. A crack of thunder came on its heels, exploding directly overhead. She could see nothing. A few drops of rain fell on her face. The storm was starting again! How far had she come? How far had she to go? She had no idea. She was disorientated by the darkness. She looked behind her, seeing nothing.

Another flash of lightning came. This one lit up the entire hillside and in that moment of awesome seeing she realised that just below her there was a cleft in the rock. It broke the water's flow, siphoned it off. In the golden light she saw it flying out into space. Saw the steps going off in the opposite direction. Into the clear.

There was no relief. Only a respite of terror. She was rigid with the knowledge of danger. She thought the steps might meet the stream again down below. In another flash of lightning she saw which way to go. She lurched forward, memorising what she had seen, measuring the distance in her mind, holding it for the brief moment in which she advanced those few yards ahead. Then darkness and disorientation claimed her again.

There was now only one thing to do. She sat down on a step, pushed her legs over the next one and on to the next, slid her bottom after it, kicked her feet out again, slid, kicked, slid. Long legs. A small memory emerged from the back of her brain. Greg liked girls with long legs. This was where they were going to do her some good. She slid them over two more steps, slid after them. Felt the seat of her trousers tear on the rough stone. Kicked forward again.

Slid. She could feel the cold rock now on the bare skin of her buttocks. She didn't feel any pain. Not yet. She had to do this or she would never get down. Worry about the damage later.

And then, all at once there was a row of car lights and she saw she was not far above the road. She swung to her feet and moved warily forward. Then the rain came down, lashing at the windscreens, forcing the cars to slow. In the lights she glimpsed the narrow, steep little walkway that led on to the road. Holding herself as near erect as she could against the deluge, she made her way down the last little flight and looking carefully to right and left, crossed the road and began to run towards the Villa Rosa.

She was safe. The exhilaration was almost more than she could contain. She dashed up the road with the wind and the rain in her face, with her soaked garments clinging to her skin and her wet hair streaming. The lightning and thunder had eased but the rain had not. She ran, using the slowly moving car lights for guidance, until she scarcely had breath to go on. As she staggered to a halt she saw she was coming abreast of the Villa Rosa. She recognised its pale bulk jutting out of the cliff on the ocean side of the road.

She switched on the single light. The roof was awash. Thank God Moira had given her her own key. She slipped out of her soaking clothes, rolled them up with her under-wear, unlocked the door with the key she had been given and slipped inside. The villa was in darkness. She switched on the lights and padded naked to the back door, opened it and threw her wet clothes onto the step, then went to her room.

She was cold now that the drama was over. Cold, tired and hungry. Reaction was setting in. Her legs were trembling, as well as her hands. She wanted to cry because she was safe. She wished she wasn't alone in the villa. She thought of Greg down in the bay on *Neptuna* waiting for Pauline to come. She wanted to cry about that.

She stepped into the shower. The water was warm and

comforting. It helped with the loneliness. She must think about what she could do. It was inconceivable that Moira would want Pauline and herself together under her roof. And Greg? Was she so utterly insensitive that she would actually entertain Greg along with both of his girls?

Then she remembered how disturbed Moira had been when she learned Greg was in the restaurant with another woman. How she had tried to shield Julie from the knowledge. But the toast they were drinking? Could it have been about something private, between themselves? She felt the hot water was softening her sharp edges.

She stayed under the shower for a long time. The bathroom was full of steam. It was billowing through to her bedroom. With a towel wrapped round her head and another round her body she padded across to the window and opened it. The rain had stopped, the sky cleared. She could see the moonlight silvery on the bay. She dried herself, pulled her robe round her and tied the sash. She noted it was the blue wrap she had been going to take on honeymoon and wondered about the moment of mental aberration that had allowed for its being packed.

What was that? She was alerted by the sound of a door opening. Surely Moira wasn't back already? Maybe she had got a taxi and come looking for her? She wrapped a fresh towel round her head and went out to face the music.

"So it's you!" said Greg, standing in the hall in dry shirt and jeans with wet hair and face. "Don't I always manage to walk in uninvited when you're here?" He grinned down at her.

She stared at him, stupefied with shock at his disloyalty, his temerity, his sheer cold-heartedness. He came forward, holding out his arms.

She found her voice breathlessly. Backed away. "I'm with Moira," she said, as if he didn't know. "Moira's here. Up at that restaurant. I came back alone."

His arms sank slowly to his sides. "And got soaked?" He glanced across at the open door. "Are those your clothes I stepped over?"

She couldn't answer him. Not coherently. She was looking at his hard, handsome face, at his smiling eyes. She burst out painfully, "She's with your friend Pauline."

It seemed to her that he laid a puzzled expression over his features like a thin shroud. They became different. Puzzled and innocent. "My friend? Moira's friend, more like. But yes, you're right, she's mine too, now," he acceded.

It was too much. Julie was breaking up inside. She felt the little pieces of her falling about as he smashed them with his lies and his cruelty. "You're just like all the others," she said, dismissing him with contempt. "You've been to Geneva with her. I rang your office. They said you were going to Geneva. And so was she. I saw her leave Moira's salon and get into your car. And now she's on *Neptuna* with you." She turned her head away, furious with herself for allowing him to see how upset she was.

Greg held out his arms again. She stared at them, hypnotised by their confidence as they extended towards her, the hands reaching. They were coming closer. She saw what they represented and ached to go into the precious haven of them for the short term comfort they would afford. Then her mind flashed ahead to the mortification that would inevitably ensue.

He was close. So close she could smell the essence of him, feel his warmth, sense his strength. She gathered up all the insults and humiliations she had suffered, put them in the palm of her hand and slapped him hard across the face. He was her parents, Oliver Wingate, Martin, Pauline and Moira as well as the debt of fifty thousand pounds. The controlled and deliberate violence was her answer to what life had dealt out to her and he was the victim because he it was who had contributed the biggest, the most intolerable measure of pain by giving her back her self-worth, then taking it away.

Blinded by her own passion and despair, she didn't see him go. She found herself back in her room, face downwards on the bed. She didn't cry. There were no tears in her. Only a terrible sense of loss. She wished she could die.

A long time later she heard a tap on the door. "Julie! You are there?"

She rolled over, stepped onto the floor and padded barefoot to the door to let her in. Moira flicked on the light. Her astonishment was written all over her face in dark eyes, parted lips, a creased and querying forehead. "You are here! Thank goodness for that! But what happened? Why did you run away? And what about the storm? You must have been caught in the storm."

Julie went to the dressing table mirror and ran a comb through her damp and tousled hair.

Moira saw her reflection in the brighter light over the glass. "You've been crying!" she exclaimed in consternation.

"No." But she was going to. At any moment. Julie backed on to the bed, crunching her trousseau wrap between her clenched fists as she drew it across her bare knees, noting its connection with Martin and what she had to do next.

Moira sat down in a little white painted bamboo chair, cushioned to match the curtains. "You got up from the table and went out. Then the storm started again. We were frantic."

"I'm sorry. Look here, Moira, I have decided to go back to Paris tomorrow and tell my father I will marry Martin. You've got Pauline for company. I'm sorry about tonight. I'm terribly sorry. It was Pauline being on *Neptuna* and coming to join us that was the final straw." No, not the final straw. That had been provided by Greg's outrageous expectations of her. Greg the two-timer, the philanderer, the lecher, the libertine. Greg who had seen her need and made her fall in love with him.

Moira heaved a sigh. "What a muddle. *Brouillamini*," she said. "Come and talk to my friend Pauline." Her voice was gentle. "She has something to say to you that would be better explained by Greg, but he is not here."

"Tell her he's back on *Neptuna*," Julie flashed, coming alive again. "I'm sorry because he's your guest, but I sent him off with a flea in his ear."

182

"A flea! I have heard of creepy creatures getting into ears, but never a flea."

"It is an English colloquialism. Don't use it. You won't get it right," Julie snapped.

Moira smiled. "A woman does not automatically get into bed with a man just because she spends the night on a boat with him. They have much to talk about."

"Didn't they talk in Geneva?"

"Now, Julie." Moira leaned forward, wagging an admonitory finger at her. "I will tell you why she's here. Because her brother-in-law is Chief of Police in Amalfi. That is why I have introduced her to Greg. An Englishman in trouble in a foreign country needs someone influential on his side. If you had come back to the table you would have found us drinking a toast to the satisfactory winding-up of this Samantha affair."

Julie looked at her stonily. She felt the coldness in her heart. She seemed to have lost all sense of trust. She did not regret it, if without trust she might obtain a sense of safety in its place.

"Why did you not return?"

"Let me ask you a question," said Julie. "Tell me why they should spend a few days in Geneva getting to know each other before Pauline introduced him to her Chief of Police."

"Julie! Please. Not so bitter, I beg of you. I cannot talk to you about their going to Geneva. It is Greg's business." She bent down and took Julie by the arm, encouraging her to rise. "Come and talk to Pauline."

Julie went reluctantly with her into the salon. She looked uncertainly at the person who was relaxed on the sofa, seeing her properly for the first time, a tall, slender woman of about thirty-plus in a navy blue tailored trouser suit with little gold buttons down the front and on the cuffs.

Moira said, drawing her two companions together in her friendly way, "Now, doesn't Pauline look like a lawyer?"

Julie thought she did but hesitated to say so in case Pauline should think, coming from a stranger, it was not a compliment.

"And you are a businesswoman," put in Pauline, looking her up and down thoughtfully. She did not hesitate to comment, "You certainly don't look like one."

Julie looked into her heart and recognised what she had not seen before. That living with her parents, taking orders from her father, there had been no opportunity to acquire the unmistakeable veneer that comes from struggling alone, battling one's way up the ladder towards success. Of course she had worked, but always knowing the rewards were there for her, held in reserve. Waiting to be picked up, at appropriate times.

"You're going to have to tell her about Geneva," put in Moira, "when you finish with the compliments – or insults as I believe I read in Julie's expression. It's too late to call Greg up. And besides, she has placed a flea inside his ear."

"I told you you'd get it wrong."

"Pauline," said Moira with a pained look. "Tell her why you went to *Génève* with Greg. I can't do anything with her. She is so cross."

Pauline said, "I'm sorry. That is Greg's business."

"He has retained you."

"But it is his business."

Moira uttered a sigh. "Let's have a nightcap. Brandy?" She went to the cupboard and brought out three fat-bellied glasses.

Julie took the glass offered to her. The brandy burnt her throat. Brought tears to her eyes. She remembered she had missed her dinner. Moira found Pauline some night clothes and they went off to bed. Julie wandered in to the kitchen. There was nothing much here for they had not bothered to shop. In the morning she would run down into the town early and get some rolls. Or perhaps they would have breakfast at one of those pavement cafés. She found some rather dry biscuits. She ate one, then another, then a third. She sat down on a stool with the biscuit tin on the bench in front of her. She thought about Greg's troubles that with Pauline's help might soon be overcome. She took another biscuit, chewed it thoughtfully thinking about the fact that he would then be free to love her. If she had not driven him away.

She took another biscuit and contemplated her own future in a *ménage à trois* with Martin and Antonia. She thought of her father in his hospital bed, inevitably baffled by the news her mother had given him, that their daughter had waved a magic wand and recreated paradise. Her fingers went back into the biscuit tin. She took another. After a while it was empty. She felt a little sick.

There was a sound of footsteps. She looked up. Moira stood in the doorway in a fabulous negligé of black silk, heavily embroidered. Her dark hair was dragged back from her forehead as usual but now it was held in place with a band and hung loosely to her shoulders. She looked younger than her thirty-five years. She came forward and looked into the biscuit tin then turned to Julie with an expression of sheer disbelief. "You ate the lot?"

Julie felt herself start to crumple.

"It is a sad state of affairs when you have to go to a tin of old biscuits for comfort."

"Yes." She looked down at the floor, not wanting to expose the unbearable misery that might be showing in her eyes.

"What happened between you and Greg tonight? This flea?"

"I sl— I—"

"Go on," said Moira encouragingly.

After a while she managed to say it. "I slapped his face."

"And a fine thing that is to do to a man who has gone out of his way to help you," exclaimed Moira indignantly. "As if he hasn't got enough troubles of his own." She ran her hands up the back of her head, fanning out the heavy hair, allowing it to drop again. "Look here," she said, "you really ought to know. I'm not supposed to tell you but you really ought to know. Greg would have told you if you hadn't – hit him? I can't believe it. I know why they went to *Génève* because I was there when Greg asked Pauline. You do know I introduced them? Maybe it is unethical for Pauline to tell you, but nobody told me not to. I can repeat what I overheard, what you really ought to know before you – in case you— Really, Julie, you do seem to have put your foot in it."

Julie looked compulsively at the biscuit tin then looked away again.

"Pauline is a friend of the man who manages your hotel in *Génève*. I was telling her about—" she stopped, looking guilty, then started again. "I was showing her the dress we had made for your wedding. You did mention selling it." She waited for Julie's reaction.

"Yes," she said. "But you'd better not, now."

"Then Greg walked in and well, he was listening, you understand. That was when Pauline asked if you were of the Creighton family who owned the hotels. She stays at Le Bosquet when she is in *Génève* because she knows the manager."

"Maurice?"

"I'm glad you found your tongue," said Moira. "You may as well take your eyes off that tin." She put the lid back on and slid it into the cupboard. "Greg asked her if she would go to Switzerland with him and introduce him to this Maurice."

"Why?"

"He wanted to help you, Julie. He could see you were up to your neck in something you couldn't cope with."

"Why Geneva?"

"Because that's where he had the introduction, don't you see? He couldn't go poking round at the London or Paris hotels, not with your mother and that man Wingate around."

And Geneva was where Oliver Wingate's money had been spent. Julie remembered the letter she had found in her father's files. Remembered, too, Martin saying the decorating was his father's idea.

"In spite of all the trouble he is in himself," said Moira severely, "he has done this for you. If your father wishes, he is prepared to retain Pauline for you to take this Wingate man to court. It's up to you."

Julie looked at Moira with tears in her eyes.

186

"I'll be able to sell the wedding dress," said Moira. "No problem. But you had better deal with this unconsidered slap yourself."

Chapter Twelve

Julie wakened to the white, clear light of early morning. Behind the villa, beyond the rocky range of mountains that guarded the coast the sun would be creeping up out of its night-time hiding place. She stood up. Looked round the room. It was seven o'clock.

She pulled a pair of jeans out of the wardrobe, a T-shirt from a drawer. Ran a comb through her hair. She listened to the silence in the villa. Slipped her feet into sandals. Unlocked the back door. Stepped over the bundle of wet clothes that lay where she had flung them and walked down the path that was still wet from the deluge of the night before. She came to the outcrop of rock where the steps began.

Colourless water lay in blurred shapes on the uneven surface. She moved warily. The sky was lightening, lifting the ink glaze from the bay but the steps were in deep shadow. Down, and down again. Now the path went horizontal. Across another outcrop of rock, then down again. She saw the tunnel ahead, bent down and hurried through. Here were the boulders that hid the beach. She skirted them and came out on the little strip of sand.

There fifty yards away was the pale outline of Greg's yacht gently rocking, with the dinghy alongside. It occurred to her that she might swim out and climb aboard, wait for Greg to appear, and apologise. She looked down at her jeans. She didn't fancy swimming in them. Why had she not brought her bikini? She should have realised the dinghy wouldn't be there. Greg would have used it last night to go aboard. She shivered. It was cold in the shadow of the mountain. She wondered if the metal ladder would be hanging over the side. Greg might take it in at night for security. She strained her eyes to see it. Couldn't remember whether it lay to port or starboard. Couldn't see it, anyway.

She might swim out in jeans and climb into the dinghy. No, she had better discard the jeans. She visualised herself sitting there, wet and forlorn, when Greg came out on deck, perhaps hours later. Saw herself looking up at him. Heard him say, curtly, "What the hell are you doing there?" Then he said, "You've got a nerve."

She sat down on the sand with her knees up under her chin. She was aware of the sand's wetness seeping through to her skin. If she was going out she really ought to get her bikini.

The veil of darkness was lifting from the bay. Far in the hazy distance she thought she could see the lion-shaped rock that was the island of Capri beginning to emerge from mist. Daylight was painting images on the water. Fishing boats at anchor. A motor boat speeding out from the shore, sharp-nosed, high-bowed. How fast the day came. She watched the bay come to life.

Her eyes returned to the yacht. It was swinging round, tugging at its anchor. The light caught the shine of metal. She ought now to be able to see the ladder if it was there. She strained her eyes. It was. She stood up. Began to unzip her jeans.

Then she saw Greg emerge from the companionway. He wore a pair of shorts and his torso was bare. He went purposefully across the deck. He was undoing the chain railing. Examining it. Then he bent down and seemed to be closely examining the deck. He sat, cross-legged and hunched over with his head lowered as though looking at something on the deck. He rose and went to the wheelhouse. Came out again. What was he doing now? He seemed to be sliding towards the edge. He stepped back. Kicked forwards again. Then he turned, disappeared down the companionway and returned walking with great care. As though he was wearing shoes. But he wouldn't wear shoes, even if he was about to go ashore, as he patently was not. Nobody ever wore shoes on the deck of a boat.

Julie kicked her jeans off and tossed them on a boulder. She waded into the water. At that moment Greg's luck ran out. His feet shot from under him and he went over the side. Julie swam fast, head down. In the lee of the boat she stopped, looking round. She called. There was no reply. Then she saw him, floating face down just a few yards away.

She struck out towards him, pushed him over on to his back and slid her arms under his as she had been taught in her lifesaving class at school. He was heavy. Almost too heavy for her to drag. She kicked hard, made a little progress towards the dinghy. Kicked. Kicked. He jerked violently and broke her hold. He was sinking. She dived. Pulled him up. Held his head above the water. He began to vomit. Sea water poured out of his mouth in a stream. His body jerked convulsively, his movements so violent and so aimless she could scarcely keep hold of him. Then he went limp and seemed about to sink again.

Once more she got a grip under his arms, pulled him towards the dinghy. She told him the dinghy was there. "Grab hold," she cried in terror. She was terrified that her strength would not last. He had to help. She was not going to manage if he didn't. "Try to get a hold," she gasped. His hand went up. Then he started to sink again.

With a superhuman effort, she raised him. The dinghy was behind her. She could feel it bumping against her head. She managed to pull him round so that he was close to it. His head and shoulders were above the level of the water again. She turned him so his back was to the dinghy. The salt water came out of his mouth in convulsive gasps. The terror went. She was aware of being immensely calm. She didn't think ahead. She knew she couldn't get him to the dinghy. She held on. Was aware of holding. Of being the lifeline between Greg and possible safety. If he went down again, if she lost him again, she thought that would be the end. She clung on to him with one arm. Held on to the dinghy with the other. She wasn't going to be able to hold out much longer. Don't let him drown. Don't let him drown.

It was put into the hands of the vigilant coastguards to

make the life or death decision. A man in white in a peaked cap came raging up beside them in his fast little motor boat. He and his companion pulled Greg aboard, hoisted him on to the deck of *Neptuna* and set about the task of pumping water out of his lungs.

"Lucky," he said. He knew a little English. "Lucky we go on early morning run."

They wanted to know if they could do anything more. Take Greg to *il medico*, for instance? The lump on his head that had stunned him as he hit the deck? What about that? Shouldn't he see *il dottore*?"

Greg answered them in Italian. That brought forth a flood Julie could not understand. Sitting on the deck supporting himself against the wall of the deckhouse he said he was OK. His head was killing him but he thought he'd survive. There was a lump the size of an egg. Well, a seabird's egg. The Signora would no doubt make him some coffee. He looked up at Julie who was standing looking down at him with her wet T-shirt clinging round her thighs and her hair dripping. She wanted to cry.

They replaced the chain railing, tut-tutting about his carelessness. Julie waited for him to explain what he had been doing. He didn't.

They thanked the men and waved them on their way. The sun had come up, a great orange ball risen above the black-shadowed mountain. It was warm on Julie's cold skin. She asked Greg if she might go below and get some dry towels and clothes.

"Help yourself." He waved her towards the companion-way. He didn't say, Put on one of my shirts, which he might have done if he had wished her to stay out of the cabin in which he kept his wife's clothes. She stood looking down at him musing on the fact that he hadn't thanked her for saving his life. Perhaps people didn't. Perhaps, life being what they were accustomed to having, they accepted it as a right. She hadn't apologised for hitting him. She didn't want to, because then both of them would have to remember it had happened.

She went down the steps and along to the tiny bathroom.

She found a coloured swimming towel deocrated with fierce looking fish with dark eyes. His towelling wrap hung behind the door, black and white stripes. Starkly masculine. She hurried back on deck and gave them to him.

"What happened?" she asked. "You must tell me. I was watching from the beach. What were you doing?"

He didn't answer immediately. Then, "I lost a good pair of shoes," he said. "I didn't do them up."

"Just as well," she said, thinking of the extra weight. "What were you doing in shoes?"

Again he didn't answer immediately. Then he said, "Go into the cabin where Samantha's clothes are and see if you can find a bluish-greenish dress. I think, short sleeves. Maybe some buttons at the front. It's not a sun-dress." He repeated, looking down at the deck, not at her, "Bluish-greenish."

She went. It was strange, looking into the cabin, having now been given permission, at the clothes that had belonged to his wife. Jammed together in the little wardrobe, because there was never much space on a boat. There were only half a dozen of them. Nothing bluish-greenish, as he had said. And they were all strappy sun-dresses, anyway. There was nothing with sleeves. She went back and told him. He didn't look up. She could not see his eyes. She turned away. Stood at the rail looking at the shore, thinking she should swim back, not wanting to leave him, thinking he wished to be alone.

"Let's have some coffee, shall we?"

She thought his need to get rid of her might be greater than his desire for coffee. She went into the little galley and found the percolator. Two mugs. Some milk. She watched the jug. The water came to the boil and she did what had to be done with it. Automatically. Not wanting to look at what had happened, at what he didn't want to tell her.

She brought the coffee up. He took a sip then put the mug down on the deck. Still without looking at her he said, "Sam didn't live by rules. If I wasn't here she would wear shoes on deck. If she came aboard to pick something up before

192

going to the plane she wouldn't have bothered to remove her shoes." He took another sip of coffee. Coughed. She thought he might be in pain from the sea water gone into his lungs. "Those shoes I put on had leather soles. I should have known if she went over feet first and hit her head there was a reasonable chance I'd do the same." He touched the lump gingerly.

"Yes."

After a moment he said, "It's not as though she couldn't swim." He seemed a million miles away. "Lucky you were there." He looked up. His face was pale behind the tan. "How?"

"I wanted to apologise."

"Oh, that," he said, dismissing it.

He looked up at the cliff. "I don't want to leave. Do you think you could row yourself ashore?"

"I'm still wet. I can swim."

"No," he said, violently, and she allowed something terrible to creep out of her mind. The fact of his certainty that Samantha lay somewhere down there. In the dark waters below the boat. No one could swim there now for fear of what they might find. He said, "There was a tiny bit of blue thread where a deck board had splintered. It was caught behind the splinter. Where I went over. Like a dress could be caught if . . ." He didn't finish the sentence.

She waited a long time. Then he looked up at her. His face had cleared. He said, "They can't charge me with murder. There's clear evidence of an accident. You're going to have to testify. Will you mind?"

"No," she said. "No, I don't mind." She was scrabbling through her mind trying to remember what he had said about that day Samantha ran away. He had been to Rome. Talking to people. He must have an alibi.

"I want you to tell Pauline about the bit of blue dress. She will know what to do."

She wanted to touch him. To show him some comfort. She felt she had not been invited to do so. That she did not belong here with his dreadful discovery, and his grieving. She climbed down the ladder, carefully, knowing it was

193

imperative she should not slip. That the water had become sacred as well as deadly. She remembered Greg saying to her in Paris, "Accidents happen all the time on boats." She saw that in death he had forgiven the wife who was running away from him when she had been claimed by the sea.

She rowed to the beach, pulled the boat up on the sand as far as she was able, put her jeans under her arm and started up the rock face.

Chapter Thirteen

Pauline and Moira dressed in double-quick time and went off to Amalfi to talk to the police, Pauline looking businesslike in a jade green two-piece; Moira in a bright blue cotton jumper and rainbow-hued scarf. Even facing disaster Moira managed to look flamboyant.

"You'd better change and then go back and wait with Greg," Moira said. "Tell him I'm going to telephone Sam's mother to find out if that dress was among her things. And I'll call her friends the Manzinis. She saw them on that last day. Lina Manzini will remember what Sam was wearing. She's the sort of woman who would."

Julie changed into jeans and jumper then went down the path towards the steps. She was glad of the excuse to go back. She had been thinking of Greg as an island. That she needed his permission to cross the sea to him. She made her way slowly down the steps hewn out of the cliff and emerged on the little beach where she had left the dinghy. He was still sitting on the deck. His knees were drawn up, his arms extending over them, his head down. She climbed aboard and rowed out.

He heard the sound of the oars in the rowlocks and came to the rail. He had changed out of the towelling robe into jeans and a T-shirt. She tossed the rope up, he made it fast and she climbed up the ladder. She gave him the messages. He nodded, then sat down again.

She stood waiting, "It might be a good thing if you talked. Do you want to talk to me?"

He reached up and pulled her down beside her. He put an arm round her. She recognised his need and was very glad she had returned. "It's different," he said, "when you

195

know. Thinking Sam had had an accident was not at all like knowing. The knowing is devastating. I keep seeing her in her pretty dress with her beautiful hair, going down." He was silent a moment then added, "And down."

"It's all over," said Julie. "That's what you have to think of. It's not happening now. It's all over for her," she repeated, painfully. "And besides, she wouldn't have known. Remember when you went over, you were stunned. You didn't feel anything, did you?" She shivered, thinking of what might have been.

"You saved my life," he said. "Thank you."

"Glad to be of help. Any time."

He smiled faintly.

They sat close together in silence. A ferry went past. After a while the disturbance on the water reached them, rocking the yacht. He picked up her hand and held it. She recognised that he did not wish to talk any more.

It was a long time before the police came in their fast little motor boat, bringing Pauline with them, and a doctor. Moira had insisted. The police talked to Greg in Italian. He showed them the threads of Samantha's dress that he had found embedded in the split in the wood. They put it carefully into an important-looking black bag. Julie went up into the bow and sat down with her long legs hanging over the side, looking across the sunny water to Capri. After a while Pauline came to say there was nothing she could do and she had better row herself ashore. They were going back to the police station. "Wait at the villa," Pauline said. "We'll be there later. I expect Moira's turned up by now."

She went off feeling forlorn. Banished. Yet knowing she did not belong with this part of Greg's life. She wondered if she should go back to Paris, then realised she could not. Greg had been to Geneva and talked to Maurice. Moira had said he was prepared to retain Pauline so that she could take Wingate to court. It was not a moment to come face to face with her mother. She was going to have to make a statement about seeing Greg go overboard. There was something she could do to help. She tied the dinghy up and climbed the steps.

Moira returned. She dropped her handbag on an occasional

196

table and flung herself down on the sofa. "I've been to see the Manzinis," she said. "Sam had lunch with them the day she disappeared. And she was wearing that blue-green dress. It was quite distinctive. I remember it myself. We rang Sam's mother in London. She says the dress was not among her things." Moira grimaced. "I suppose they'll send divers down now. Not very nice," she said. "Not nice at all. But at least it looks as though the matter is going to be cleared up. Now, have you eaten?"

Julie shook her head.

"You are getting so thin," Moira scolded. "You wouldn't fit that wedding dress now. It would hang on you."

"I hope I'm not going to need it. If, as you say, Greg is going to help."

"Greg's up to his eyes," she replied tersely. "Let's go out and find some lunch." Julie recognised that Moira's nerves were on edge.

It was evening before Greg and Pauline returned. Marine divers had already been put to work and would resume again first thing in the morning. They knew where to search, according to the winds and the tides. Greg was quiet. Distant. They went out together down into the town, found a restaurant and ate their dinner in near silence, then came back together walking slowly up the hill to the Villa Rosa. Moira had made up beds for Greg and Pauline. None of them wanted to sit up and talk.

It was the same the next day. They inhabited a vacuum while they waited. Greg wanted to go out with the divers. They wouldn't let him. He disappeared for hours at a time. Nobody asked where he went and he didn't explain. Walking? Driving? They accepted he wanted to be alone.

In the evening he came back and they had dinner together. Afterwards, they sat around in the salon. It was a night for outdoors but that meant looking over the sea where Samantha lay. None of them mentioned it. They tried not to look at the water. For that reason the villa became claustrophobic.

Greg had brought a bottle of whisky up from *Neptuna*. He found some glasses. They recognised he did not want to go to bed so they sat with him. Moira poured some wine. There were only two shaded lights in the big room. It had obtained a cave-like dimness. They talked desultorily, each beginning taking a different subject.

"Remember that weekend in Rome, Greg? Six years ago? Remember the awful hotel? And you got drunk and we wouldn't let you drive the car?"

So they had been friends more than six years. Julie thought, I know so little about them and yet we have grown so close. So attached.

Greg raised his glass to his lips. "It was Andrew's fault. He told me afterwards. We had run out of whiskey. He added some gin to my glass."

"You never said."

"No. You'd have given him a rocket, wouldn't you?"

"I would indeed."

"I remember a case," said Pauline. "One of my very first. Drunk driving." She didn't continue and nobody asked her to go on.

"How will you know where you were at the time?" Moira asked and because their minds had not left the subject they all knew she was referring to the day Samantha went overboard.

"I keep a diary. I have to."

Julie wondered if he was keeping note of his movements. Or Samantha's movements. Or his business meetings. Whether his diary was on his desk. Or in his pocket. She thought of her own appointments book on her desk in Paris. Of Melusine whom she had left to cope. Her thoughts see-sawed back and forth.

Moira said, "The geraniums didn't survive the downpour."

Pauline yawned. As though it was a signal, they drifted off to bed.

Next day the divers found a blue-green hat, battered and torn, scarcely recognisable after months in the water but still miraculously retaining the name of the Paris milliner Samantha patronised. It was wedged tightly between some rocks.

They were more settled that evening. Proof had come. Though Greg had known ever since he found the threads

198

of Samantha's dress, knowing wasn't proof. They were easier with one another that day. And closer. They dared to leave the villa for a few hours, together. Greg took the wheel of Moira's car and they drove inland. Found a restaurant where the tables were set in tree shade. Afterwards Greg and Julie went for a walk. Greg held her hand. She felt he had given himself permission.

That evening they found an unpretentious restaurant tucked away at the back of the town. Nobody said they were searching out places where Greg and Moira would not be known and where their friends were unlikely to go. They shared the pavement tables with artisans and fishermen. "You get very good food at this sort of place," Greg said. "The locals know."

The search dragged on.

Two days later they found Samantha's body wedged, as the hat had been, in a crevasse where the wind had blown it and the shifting sea had tucked it secretly away. Greg went down to identify her. They waited for him in the street, not talking. Walked back with him. Moira slipped an arm through his. Julie wished she had been brave enough to do it, but Greg's face was so closed she felt, not rebuffed, but outside. He had become an island again. Still, he allowed Moira's closeness. They returned to the villa in a state of exhausted calm. Moira opened the back door. Not opened, Julie thought, she flung it wide.

"Let's go out into the garden for our apéritifs," she said.

They shared the wooden bench and a couple of chairs, looking out to sea. It was as though the water had lost its sacred quality now Samantha had come ashore and they could look on it again. "It's a lovely evening," said Pauline. The evenings had been lovely since the storm but their thoughts had been turned in, their eyes blind.

Moira heaved a huge sigh and addressed Julie, "To think I brought you here for a respite from your troubles."

"Her presence has been valuable," said Greg. He reached across the space between them and took Julie's hand. "She saved my life."

Julie thought it was a measure of what they had been through that the saving of Greg's life had been merely 'valuable'.

"And it's just as well," Greg added, "because I don't know how she would have got out of her troubles without me."

It seemed with that sentence he had put the past behind him and was looking ahead. Seeing a challenge in the future.

Moira said briskly, "Pauline and I wish to have dinner on our own tonight. So we'll leave you two to make separate arrangements." Pauline quickly hid her surprise. They rose and went into the villa.

Julie and Greg sat in silence, still holding hands, watching the sun go down and the stars come out. Over on the horizon the great crouching lion rock of Capri emerged from its evening mist and grew black against the scarlet and gold of the sky.

"It's been a bad beginning," said Greg. "So bad I'm having difficulty believing it's come right in the end."

Julie put two fingers against his lips. "It's true. Don't think about it. Just accept that it's true. Can we go to that restaurant where we went the night we met?"

"Where, against all the odds, we fell in love, me thinking you were a spoiled brat, and in love with another man."

"Where I fell in love with you, in spite of having heard you took to me only because you are attracted to girls with long legs, neat features and long fair hair."

He looked astonished. "Who told you that?"

"I overheard it."

He laughed. "There may be something in it. They say a man often marries a girl who looks like his mother. Or his sisters. They answer that description. Yes, you may be right. You may have told me something about myself. You know so little about me, dear Julie. I feel I've known you forever. Been kept from helping you forever. There's so much I could have done, if only I had been – shall we say – respectable? If I hadn't been living under a cloud. I haven't even been able to talk to you properly."

200

"You went to Geneva and talked to Maurice."

"Pauline told me he was looking for another job."

"What?" And then she remembered the near-mutiny in the Paris hotel and thought she should not have been surprised.

"I knew this would be the last straw for you. I was on my way here. It was easy enough to drop by and see what it was about. I interfered," said Greg. "He's holding on, at my request. I told him I was acting on your behalf. Not quite true, but I felt you wouldn't mind. It's all about Wingate sending in his decorator. He thinks your father isn't in control any more. Wasn't, even before the heart attack."

"Oh Greg! With so much on your mind you did this for me?"

"It gave me something to think about. Besides, I like a good fight. And I could see you weren't going to be able to cope. You haven't a chance against Wingate, on your own, you know. Would you like to go and see your father?"

"He's not allowed to talk business."

"I think I know how to deal with that," said Greg.

She thought, he has such confidence. And isn't that what I need? "Yes," she said, "I would like you to go and see him."

"Why don't we hop across to Geneva on the way home? I'd like you to see what's been done. It's not irreversible. Pauline thinks Wingate could be made to put it back the way it was."

She nodded. She felt the release of all the strain of the last few weeks. 'Perhaps in the sun your troubles will melt away,' Moira had said. She felt, in a sense, they had. At least they had moved to Greg's broad shoulders. She thought, I gave his life back to him. Now perhaps he will be able to give my father his life, which is his peace of mind.

They walked together up the hill hand in hand beneath the starlit sky. The wild orange blossom weighted the air with perfume, the moon sent a silvery trail across the sea. Far in the distance, a group of golden lights like glow-worms showed where the fishing boats lay. They climbed the narrow stone steps and came to the restaurant. The same little lights glowed in the darkness. The same tables were set out in the cloisters.

The head waiter came. "*Buon giorno*. You wish the table beneath the bougainvillea?"

"No other one would do," said Greg. "This is a very special celebration."

"You celebrate last time." The waiter beamed as Italians will when there is romance in the air.

"A rather better celebration than the last one."

"Okay." He bustled ahead of them. "There will be champagne?"

"And he will bring me a hibiscus," said Julie smiling as she sat down at the small table where they had first learned a little about each other. "This really is where we came in, isn't it?"